Kenneth Mcalpine
A Tale Of Mountain, Moorland And Sea

by
Gordon Stables

Kenneth Mcalpine
A Tale Of Mountain, Moorland And Sea
by Gordon Stables

Copyright © 2024

All Rights reserved.

No part of this publication may be reproduced, stored in a retrieval system, or transmitted in any form or by any means, electronic, mechanical, photocopying or Otherwise, without the written permission of the publisher.
The author/editor asserts the moral right to be identified as the author/editor of this work.

ISBN: 978-93-62766-49-6

Published by

DOUBLE 9 BOOKS
2/13-B, Ansari Road
Daryaganj, New Delhi – 110002
info@double9books.com
www.double9books.com
Tel. 011-40042856

This book is under public domain

ABOUT THE AUTHOR

Gordon Stables turn out to be a prolific nineteenth-century Scottish author, physician, and naval officer, whose works regularly revolved spherical maritime and journey troubles. One of his exceptional creations, "Wild Adventures spherical the Pole," continues to seize the imaginations of readers. Published inside the late 19th century, this e-book is a thrilling and innovative story of polar exploration. "Wild Adventures round the Pole" takes readers on a charming adventure to the Arctic, where Stables weaves a story filled with daring exploits, breathtaking landscapes, and encounters with the cruel realities of the frozen frontier. Gordon Stables' writing is understood for its shiny descriptions and his deep knowledge of the seafaring lifestyles. His reviews as a naval officer lent authenticity to his maritime narratives, permitting readers to feel the loosen up of the polar winds and the push of excitement as explorers braved the unknown. Stables' works often convey strong moral undertones, emphasizing courage, camaraderie, and the indomitable human spirit in the face of adversity. "Wild Adventures round the Pole" is not any exception, as it encourages readers to undertaking into the uncharted territories of their very personal lives with a feel of marvel and resolution.

CONTENTS

Chapter One
Early Days 7

Chapter Two
Kenneth and his Friends 17

Chapter Three
The Story of the Fairy Knoll 28

Chapter Four
Gloaming in the Glen—Kennie's Cave 37

Chapter Five
A Day in the Wilds 46

Chapter Six
Kenneth 55

Chapter Seven
The Death of Poor Nancy 62

Chapter Eight
Kenneth and Jessie 69

Chapter Nine
The Storm Cloud Bursts over the Glen 75

Chapter Ten
The Last Link is Broken 82

Chapter Eleven
For Auld Lang Syne 86

Chapter Twelve
Kenneth and Archie 93

Chapter Thirteen
Kenneth's Story (continued)—At the Cave 104

Chapter Fourteen
Friday Night at Sea 111

Chapter Fifteen
Christmas Day in the Doldrums 118

Chapter Sixteen
Frozen up in the North 122

Chapter Seventeen
A Tale Told on the Sea of Ice 130

Chapter Eighteen
On the Unknown River 136

Chapter Nineteen
The Search for the Land of Gold 144

Chapter Twenty
Land of Darkness 152

Chapter Twenty One
Camp-Life in the Far West 160

Chapter Twenty Two
Glen Alva under New Government 168

Chapter Twenty Three
The Wanderer's Return 174

Chapter Twenty Four
In the "Fa' o' the Year" 181

Chapter One
Early Days

"Away, ye gay landscapes, ye garden of roses,
And bring me the land where the dewdrop reposes."

Byron.

"Poor woolly mother, be at peace!
Whither thou goest I will bear thy care."

M. Arnold.

Scene: A Highland mountain, clad almost to the summit in purple heather. On the right a ravine, half hidden by drooping birch trees. On the left a pine forest. Sheep grazing in the foreground. Smoke upcurling from a humble cottage in the distance. A shepherd-boy talking to his dog; between them a lamb is lying on the ground.

"It is dead, Kooran, dead, dead, dead. It is as dead as ever a lamb was, Kooran. Ay, my doggie, I ken you're sorrowful and anxious, but you may stand there and lick its little face and legs, till this time the morn, Kooran, but you can never bring back life to it again.

"What do you say, Kooran? Its eyes are still bright and shinin' and life-like? True; but wait a wee, Kooran. Yes, wait a wee, dear frien'. In less than an hour, Kooran, its poor eyes will be glassy enough, and its bits o' legs as cold and stiff as the crook I'm holding in my hand.

"Let us hide it awa' in under this bush o' whins,—out o' sight of the poor woeful mother of it. I canna bear to bury it just yet, while the heart is still warm, but by-and-bye, Kooran; by-and-bye, doggie.

"Yonder comes the mother, Kooran. She has left the flock again."

The sheep bleats.

"Listen, Kooran, listen. What a mournfu' bleat! It makes my blood creep. And look at her eyes, Kooran. They seem starting out o' the sockets wi' excitement. Drive her back, Kooran, but *walk*, doggie; dinna run. Drive her ever so gently. She'll never have her lammie to trot at her heels again. Gently, Kooran, gently.

"And now, Kooran, off you trot home for the barley scones and the flagon o' milk. I'll have the lammie buried before you come back, so the sight of that will trouble you no more. Then we'll have dinner, doggie, and it is time, too. Look at the sun where it is, right over the highest peak of Ben Varra. Off you trot, Kooran, and dinna let the grass grow under your feet till you're back again.

"Heigho! another lammie dead!" The boy was alone now; the faithful dog had departed at once on his mission. In a bee-line down the mountain's side went he, feathering along through the grass and the patches of blooming heather, jumping over boulders, and springing down from rocky ledges with a daring that would assuredly have proved fatal to any other kind of dog, save a Highland collie or a Scottish deerhound. Finally he went splashing through a broad though shallow river, and immediately after disappeared in a clump of those sweet-scented birch trees that grow so plentifully in "the land of the mountain and flood."

"Heigho! another lammie dead!"

The boy had gone farther up the hill, and as he spoke he threw himself down on top of a couch made of heather, dislodging as he did so several mossy bees that had come to suck the honey from the little purple bells.

Quite a work of art was this couch. It had taken the boy all the livelong morning and forenoon to make it, Kooran meanwhile trotting about after him or standing by his side, with one ear pricked up, the other down, very much interested indeed in the progress of the work, and apparently sorry that he was only a dog and could not lend a hand.

Wouldst know how this couch was built? First and foremost, then, the lad had sought out a proper site, flat and smooth, on which to make it.

This was chosen close to a steep-rising rock far up the mountain's side, and whence he could see not only all the country far and wide, but the grazing ground of his flock of sheep some distance down beneath him.

Under the rock, but fully exposed to the rays of the summer sun, for Kenneth was not a bit afraid of spoiling his complexion. Indeed, such an accident would have been impossible, for neither his face nor his knees—he wore the Highland garb—could have been one whit browner than they were. And as for the sun giving him a headache, that was out of the question—the sun's rays had not the power. For when taking a *siesta*, as shepherd lads are wont to do sometimes, his favourite attitude was lying on his back with one arm under his head and his face upturned to the god of day, for he feared the sun no more than does yonder eagle that goes circling up and up towards it, even as moths, on a summer's evening, go wheeling round and round the lamp flame.

A black, bare, bleak-looking rock it was, but canopied over with the greenest of green moss and trailing saxifrages, bearing tiny flowerets of pink and white and blue.

Quite a work of art was this heather couch, and as perfect as any one could wish to see it. Not from any place near to the rock, however, had the boy pulled the heather with which he formed it. There was something of the poet and the artist about the lad, and he would never have dreamt of spoiling the gorgeous purple carpet that grew on the hill immediately in front of and beneath him. He went farther afield and higher up for his couch material. And he *cut* it close off by the roots, for if you *pull* heather, then with the roots are sure to come up both moss and turf.

When he had culled quite an armful, he proceeded to tie it up into little bundles or sheaves, and so on sheaf after sheaf he manufactured, singing to himself or talking to Kooran, until he had quite enough to build his heather sofa withal.

Then he took all his sheaves down to the rock and commenced operations, placing them side by side close together with the bloom uppermost, and lo and behold, in less than half an hour, a couch soft and fragrant enough for the dainty limbs of some fairy queen to recline upon.

It was on this heather bed, then, that Kenneth threw himself at full length as soon as Kooran had disappeared in the distant birch wood.

For fully a quarter of an hour Kenneth lay looking up at the white-grey clouds, that were scudding swiftly across the blue of the beautiful sky. He was wishing he could be up there, up riding on yonder cloud, away from the earth entirely. "Just for a time, oh! only for a time," he muttered; "I would come back to my sheep and Kooran. Yonder is a laverock," (lark). "I can hardly see it, it has flown so high but I can hear it, and how bonnie it sings as it flutters its wings, and seems to fan the very clouds. Let me see what the song says. But no, I mustn't sing, and I mustn't read. Kooran will soon be back wi' the dinner, and I haven't buried the poor lammie yet."

So saying, he jumped up. He had a spade handy. Alas! much to Kenneth's sorrow, that spade had been used many times too often this summer, for it had been a bad season among the sheep. He got the spade, and carried that and the dead lamb far up above the spot where he had cut the heather. Here the mountain was split as it were in two, or rather there were two hills, with a green strath or glen between, formed thousands of years or ages agone, by the gradual descent of some mighty glacier.

The glade was green and in many places soft, though by no means boggy. Near a bush Kenneth quickly dug a grave, and with a sigh he laid the lamb therein, and covered it up, laying the sod down again, so that it was scarcely discernible from the turf around it.

Then he shouldered his spade and prepared to go back. But remembering something else, he made a détour and came at last to a patch of whins.

Hidden in a cosy corner close to the ground was a nest well lined with feathers, and the little bird popped stealthily out as he approached.

"Oh! the beauties," cried the boy, "the bonnie wee 'hoties,'" (a kind of finch). "There were four white and red eggs when I saw you last, and there lie four naked gorbles, gaping up at me with wide yellow mouths. Now that nest is easily seen, and if other boys find it when I'm no' here, they'll kill the young and break the mither's heart. I'll try and hide it. It's maybe the last nest I'll find this season." As he spoke he looked about, and soon found a branchlet of withered whins, which he placed carefully in front of the nest, then took up his spade again and was about to withdraw, when his eyes lighted on one of those curious green knolls, that are common enough in some bare mountain glens in the Scottish Highlands.

"A fairy hill!" he said half aloud. "I do wonder now if there are such things as fairies, and if on moonlight nights they come oot, and dance on this green hillock. Oh! wouldn't I like to see them just! I've a good mind to come and watch here some bonnie night. I could bring Kooran; I wouldna be feared if Kooran was with me."

He climbed up to the top of the green knoll as he spoke. It was perfectly round and smooth, and the grass grew softer and greener here than anywhere else in all the glade. "Why," he said, "here is a hole near the top for all the world like a lum," (chimney). "Is it possible, I wonder, that fairies do live inside?"

Down he went now and commenced marching round and round the knoll, prodding it everywhere as he went with his long sharp spade. The spade sank deep each time he thrust it in, until he came round to the upper side, and here it rang against a stone.

The boy went to work with a will, and soon laid that stone bare. It was merely a large flat slab and quite loose. Kenneth leapt up above it, and using the spade as a lever, he prised it up, and over it fell, revealing to the boy's astonished gaze the entrance to a dark cave. Here was indeed a discovery, and a discovery, too, that dovetailed most completely and perfectly with this lad's romantic nature.

"Well," he said, "this *is* something to think about at last. But I must go to dinner now. Kooran must come with me to explore."

He left his spade and went away singing down the glade, and back to his heather couch.

But Kooran had not returned, so the lad, giving a look first to see that the sheep were all right, lay down and took out a volume of songs and commenced to read. Poetry, however, had lost its charm to-day, for his mind would, in spite of all he could do, revert to that dark cave in the fairy knoll. So he threw down the book and gave himself up to the pleasant occupation of castle-building.

NOONTIDE ON THE MOORLAND.

The day was warm and sultry, the bees were humming lazily from heather bloom to heather bloom, and high up against the fleecy cloudlets the laverock still fluttered and sang; no wonder Kenneth's eyelids drooped, and that he soon lost himself in dreams of fairyland.

Kenneth's mother lived in the long low turf-thatched cottage beyond the birch wood. He had neither sister nor brother, and for many a long year his father had been quietly sleeping in the humble little churchyard that surrounded the ruins of the old parish kirk.

"Oh, Kooran, doggie, here you are," cried Kenneth's mother as the dog came trotting in, open-mouthed and gasping with the race he had had. "Here ye are, and I haven't milked the cow yet. But I won't be long, laddie."

Kooran signified his intention of waiting, and threw himself down on the kitchen floor, but not before he had lapped up all the cat's milk. Pussy jumped down from the three-legged stool, near the peat fire, and began purring and rubbing herself against Ivooran's chin. The cat and dog were the best of friends; perhaps pussy thought it was good policy to keep in with Kooran.

As soon as Kenneth's mother had milked the cow, she filled a tin flagon with the rich white fluid, made up a large parcel of buttered scones and cheese, tied the whole in a large red napkin, and put it on the floor.

Kooran was up and off before the cat could have winked, had she wanted to wink.

He took time to recross the stream and held the parcel high up as he did so, but he did not let the grass grow under his feet, ere he returned to the spot where he had left his young master. He was not there, but Kooran soon found him asleep on the fragrant heather couch. The dog dropped the bundle, sat down and looked at his master, and considered. This did not wake him, so Kooran gave vent to an impatient whine or two. As even that did not wake the sleeping boy, the dog licked his cheek, then clawed at his arm with his paw, and finally Kenneth sat up, rubbed his eyes, and then burst out laughing.

"What silly dreams I've had," he said, proceeding to undo the knot on the napkin, "such silly dreams! But go and fetch your dish, doggie."

Kooran trotted off, and was back again in a moment with a tin saucer, and the scones and milk were shared.

"But oh! Kooran," continued the boy presently, "I've such news for you."

The dog pricked his ears, and turning his head a little on one side, looked wondrous wise.

"No," said Kenneth, "it isn't rats, and it isn't rabbits. There is never anything else in your noddle, Kooran, but rats and rabbits. It's a cave, Kooran. Of course you don't know what a cave is, but here,—there is some more dinner for you. Eat that, and then we'll go and explore."

The boy and his dog started off up the glen immediately after, and Kooran, knowing there was something on the *tapis*, commenced to frisk and bark around his young master.

"That won't do, Kooran," said the boy, shaking his finger at his companion. "Ye mustna do that. Look down there at the sheep; every single one o' them has stopped eating to snuff the air. Come to heel and keep quiet."

They soon reached the fairy knoll, and as soon as Kooran saw the hole, his mind still running on rats and rabbits, he disappeared inside.

Never a rat nor rabbit was there, but several unwholesome-looking bats came whirring out, and dazzled by the sunlight, dropped into the first bush they came to. Kenneth himself now entered the cave, spade in hand, and as soon as his eyes got used to the darkness, he began to examine it thoroughly. It was large and roomy, the walls and floor of solid stone, with marks of tools thereon, as if the place had either been wholly excavated or enlarged by human hands. The light glimmered down the chimney and fell on some large round brown article. It was a huge kettle. Then, young though he was, Kenneth knew that at some time or other this cave had been occupied not by fairies, but by a gang of smugglers.

"It was wise of them," thought Kenneth, "to use a place like this."

Well might he think so, for even to this day, in remote districts of the Highlands, so much of superstition clings around these fairy knolls that no peasant would dare to go near them after nightfall.

Now there is one thing in which Scotland and Germany have long resembled each other. The very poorest people belonging to the two countries have from time immemorial been taught to read and write. Kenneth had had the advantages of an education far superior to most lads of his class and age. He had spent many a long year at the parish school and evening school, his mother had taught him, the clergyman's daughter had helped him, but, better than all this, he had helped himself.

When talking, as must have already been perceived, he sometimes made use of Scotch words and phrases. He did so, not because he could not speak pure English, but simply because they are often more expressive than the Saxon idiom.

"Well, Kooran," said Kenneth, "this is the best find ever we made. Dinna ye think so, doggie?"

But Kooran's nose was turned up to the roof, and his eyes wide with excitement, for he perceived, clinging by its claws up there, the strangest-looking rat ever he had seen in his life before. A rat, and still not a rat, for it had wings; yes, and it could fly, too, for even as he gazed it let go its hold and made straight for the doorway. Kooran was far too quick for it, though. He sprang up, and next moment it lay half-dead apparently between his two forepaws.

KOORAN AND HIS CHARGE : HOMEWARD BOUND.

"Strangest thing ever I came across," Kooran appeared to observe as he looked wonderingly up into his young master's face. "Rats flying; this *must* be a fairy knoll, and I feel half afraid."

"That's a bat, Kooran, a bat, boy, and you mustn't touch it. Look at its two rows of white and glittering wee teeth. Poor little thing! Kooran, it is well-nigh dead. And this cave really belongs by rights to that bat and his brothers. We'll tie it up in the napkin, and you shall carry it home, and mother will cure it and let it fly off again."

As he spoke the boy suited the action to his words.

"Yes, Kooran, this is a grand discovery. After reading 'Robinson Crusoe' so often, I've always wished to have an island all to myself; but a cave, Kooran, is nearly as good as an island. I wonder what Dugald McCrane will say about it. I'm sure he will help me to make things to furnish it, and we'll have our dinner here, Kooran, and a fire when the weather grows cold, and everything so jolly. Come, we must go this very evening and see Dugald McCrane."

True to his word, when Kenneth had driven his sheep into their fold for the night, and had eaten his supper at his mother's fireside, then, instead of taking down his books and lying down on the great wooden dais to read by the light of the little black whale-oil lamp, with its wicks of peeled and dried rushes, he got up whistled to Kooran, and said to his mother,—

"I'm going down the glen, mother."

"Dinna be lang, laddie, dinna be lang," was all his mother said.

It was a clear moonlight night, all the brighter stars were shining, and there was hardly a cloud to be seen.

Kenneth had two long Scotch miles to walk, down into a thicket of fir trees first, across a rustic bridge, under which the brown stream was dashing and swirling and ever and anon breaking itself into foam against the boulders. It was very dark down here, but Kenneth was soon away out into the open country again, and the roar of the river was no more heard. By-and-bye the road led through a wood of oak, ash, and elm trees, with now and then the dark head of a pine tree shooting high up into the sky. The moonlight showed in patches here all along the road, there was the sound of falling water not far off, mingling with the whispering of the wind among the leaves, now crisp with the sunshine of the long bright summer, and there was occasionally the mournful cry of the brown owl, which made Kenneth feel lonesome and "eerie," and he was not sorry when he was clear of that dark gloomy wood, and saw up on a hillside the light shining yellow through the blind of Keeper McCrane's cottage.

A black retriever came rushing down, growling and showing his teeth, but when he saw it was Kenneth he wagged his bell-rope of a tail, and bade him and Kooran welcome.

Kenneth left his dog in the garden to dance and caper about with the retriever. No doubt Kooran told this black dog all about the flying rats. Kenneth just opened the door and walked straight in.

Both Dugald and his young wife jumped up from their seats beside the fire, and welcomed Kenneth, and their only boy, a wonderful little fellow of some nine or ten summers old, with hair not unlike in colour to a bundle of oaten straw, got out of bed and ran to pull Kenneth by the jacket, without waiting to dress.

Dugald and his wife and boy all listened with wondering eyes to the story of the fairy knoll.

"Bless me, dear laddie," said Mrs McCrane, "were you no' afraid to venture in?"

"I'll tell you what we'll do," said the keeper. "We'll go up the glen and see the old witch wife, Nancy Dobbell. She can tell us all about it. They tell me she knows everything that ever happened for a hundred years back and more."

"Will she no' be in bed?" said his wife.

"In bed?" said Dugald. "Not she. She never goes to bed till 'the wee short hour ayont the twal,' and there is no saying what she may be doing till then."

"Well, let us go," cried Kenneth, starting up.

One glance at the walls of the room in Dugald's cottage, that did duty as both kitchen and dining-hall, would have given a stranger an insight into both the character and calling of the chief inmate. Never a picture adorned the room, but dried grasses and ferns did duty instead, and here were the skins of every kind of wild animal and bird to be found in the wilds of the Scottish Highlands, the foumart or polecat, the whitterit or weasel, the wild cat and fox, ptarmigan, plovers of every kind, including the great whaup or curlew, hawks, owls, and even the golden-headed eagle itself stood stuffed in a corner, with glaring fiery eyes and wings half outspread.

"Come," said Dugald.

And away went the keeper and Kenneth, the two dogs following closely at their masters' heels, as if to protect them from all harm.

Chapter Two
Kenneth and his Friends

"Still o'er these scenes my memory wakes,
And fondly broods with miser care;
Time but the impression deeper makes,
As streams their channels deeper wear."

Burns.

Scene: A long, low-thatched cottage, in the midst of a wild, bleak moorland. No other hut nor house in sight. Around the cottage is a garden or kail-yard, with a fence of flat, slab-like stones. In this is a gate half open, and hanging by one hinge. The cottage has its door in the gable, and is windowless, save for some holes 'twixt thatch and eaves, through which light is now glimmering. A bright round moon is riding in the sky, among a few white clouds, that look like wings. Coming towards the gateway, two figures may be seen, both in the Highland garb. Behind them two dogs.

"Losh! man," said Dugald McCrane, "I'm almost 'feared to gang farther. Who knows what company she may have in this lonesome dreary spot? Hark! What was that?"

Dugald started and stared about him in some trepidation as the prolonged and mournful shriek of an owl rose on the night air.

"It is only an owl," said Kenneth, laughing.

"Ach! man," said Dugald, "it is not me that's afraid of an owlet, but goodness be about us, Kenneth, there are owls *and* owls. Hush! there it goes again. Losh! look how the dogs are shaking and trembling?"

FRONTISPIECE.

It was true what Dugald had said; both the retriever and collie had thrown themselves at their masters' feet, and gave every indication of mortal dread. After all, it was merely owing to a kind of magnetic influence which fear always has. This had been communicated from Dugald to his dog, and from the retriever to the collie.

"It's nothing," said Kenneth, "nothing, Dugald. I'm not afraid, if you are."

"Fear!" replied the stalwart Highland keeper. "Dugald never feared the face o' clay. But look how they're shakin' yet. These dogs hear voices we cannot listen to and live; they see things that human eyes, dare not scan. Dinna deny it, Kenneth, lad; dinna seek to deny it.

"Do you remember, Kenneth, that dreary, dark December night two years ago, when Walie's wife—goodness be about us—went and hanged herself in the woods o' Alva, and how Shot there sat a' the livelong night on the top of the old turf wall and howled so mournfully? It made me tremble in my bed to hear him. And did you no' tell me that your Kooran did the same one night the year before last, and that next morning a hat and a stick were found on the brink o' Beattie's mill-dam, and poor Jock Grey's body stark and stiff—"

"Stop! stop!" cried Kenneth. "This is no time of night for such stories. Kooran, come on."

And the boy began to lead the way up through the garden to Nancy's door.

"Just a moment," said Dugald, laying a hand on Kenneth's shoulder. "Have you got your flute?"

"Yes."

"Well, just give us a toot. If Nancy has company that's no' canny, it will give them time to bolt up the chimney. Sirs! Sirs!"

Kenneth laughed, put his flute together, and started a merry air.

"The Campbells are coming; hurrah, hurrah?" was the tune he played.

Dugald forgot his fear, and began to sing. The "twa dogs" forgot theirs, and began to dance and caper and bark, and in the very middle of this "rant" the cottage door opened, and Nancy herself appeared.

"Come in, come in, you twa daft laddies," she cried, "or 'deed you'll start Nancy hersel' to dance, for as auld as she is. Come in; you'll leave the dogs outside, winna ye, for fear o' my poor cat?"

"Ay, Grannie," said Dugald, "we'll leave the dogs outside, and I'm thinkin' neither o' them would show face inside your door if you asked them e'er so kindly. My Shot there hasn't forgotten the salute your cat gave him last time he came here. If you mind, Grannie, she jumped on his back and rode him a' round the kail-yard, and never missed him a whack, till he flew out o' the gate and ran helter-skelter o'er the moor. I dinna think your cat's canny, Grannie."

"What a beautifu' nicht!" said Grannie; "but come in, laddies."

"You're sure you have no company?" said Dugald, still hesitating to enter.

"Come, ye stoopid loon," she replied. "There's nobody here but me and the cat. Sit doon. Tak' a stool, Kennie, my bonnie boy."

A bonnie boy? Yes, there was no denying it. Kenneth, our hero, was a bonnie boy, and gave promise of growing up into a fine handsome man.

"IT WAS THE BROAD ATLANTIC OCEAN."

His broad blue bonnet was usually worn pretty far back, but even had he worn it forward, I do not think it would have been possible for it to suppress the wealth of dark short curls that rose up over his broad brown brow. His cheeks had the tint that health, the winds, and the sun had given them. His lips were rosy, and when he laughed he showed a set of teeth even and white, and a merry twinkle went upwards and danced about his dark, dark eyes. But at all other times those eyes were somewhat dreamy withal. Such was Kenneth McAlpine, and it was probably that same dreamy, thoughtful look in his eyes that made him appear older than he really was, for he had not yet seen his thirteenth year.

But there was one other reason to account for Kenneth's looking somewhat older than his years. He had already come through a good deal of grief.

His father had once been a prosperous crofter or small farmer. Not that the crofts in Glen Alva were very large or very wealthy, but, when well cultivated, the land was grateful and yielded up its fruits abundantly.

Then the sea was not very far away, only a few miles, and fish therein were abundant and to be had only for the catching.

It was the broad Atlantic Ocean whose waves broke and thundered ceaselessly on the rocky shore just beyond the hills yonder. Only two years ago—what long, long years they had seemed to Kenneth!—this lad had used to spend many an hour by the seashore. Indeed, every hour that he could spare from school, or from home, he spent with the ocean.

I am quite right in saying *with* the ocean instead of *by* the sea, for Kenneth looked upon the sea as a friend and as a companion; he used to speak with it and talk to it; it seemed to understand him, and he *it*. What baskets of glorious fish he used to get from the sea! and what dozens of splendid steel blue lobsters and lordly crabs!

Kenneth used to fish from the rocks on days when he could not borrow old Duncan Reed's cobble. Old Duncan was frail and rheumatic, and could not always go out to fish himself, but one way or another he had taught Kenneth nearly all he knew about the sea and fishing. He had taught him to row, and to scull, and to make and bait and busk a line, and to swim as well.

The making of a good strong line used to be a great pleasure to Kenneth. It was manufactured from horsehair. There was first and foremost the getting of this horsehair, for quite a quantity was required. It consisted of combings from the manes and tails of horses, and many a mile Kenneth used to pad to procure it. The main source of supply was the stables of a noble lord who lived in a great old-fashioned castle miles from Glen Alva. For the horsehair so obtained Kenneth used to give to the stablemen largess in fish. Then, having obtained his supply and carried it home, it was quite a long and tedious process to plait the line. But Kenneth knew no such word as tire, so he worked and worked away at early morning and late at night, and as yard after yard of the line was made, it was rolled upon a reel roughly hewn from a branch of the silvery birch, and probably at the end of a fortnight the line would be complete, and away Kenneth would rush like a young deer over the hills.

Nancy's house on the moor lay between him and the shore, and however great a hurry Kenneth was in, he did not fail to call and speak a few moments with the "old witch wife," as she was universally called, the truth being that she was no more a witch than you or I, reader, only she was an herbalist, and wise in many other ways.

Yes, Kenneth would always find time to call at old Nancy's hut, and he never left the house without a drink of milk or whey—for Nancy kept a cow—or a cupful of heather ale. Nancy was famed far and near for making heather ale, and on Sundays the lads and lasses from a good way round, used to make a pilgrimage to Nancy's and taste her wondrous brew.

OLD DUNCAN'S COTTAGE.

Many a word of good advice Nancy had for Kenneth, too, her bonnie boy, and many a blessing.

He would soon arrive at the old fisherman's hut, which was a boat turned upside down and let into a crevice of the rocks high enough up to prevent green seas from swamping it, although in stormy weather, with a west wind blowing, the spray used to dash right over the roof.

"On days like these," old Duncan used to say, "I don't need to put any salt in my porridge, for the sea-bree that drops down the chimney makes it salt enough."

When Duncan got Kenneth's horsehair line, he used to unroll it and try the strength of it, foot by foot and yard by yard, and if it bore the test, then Duncan would put his hand on the lad's head and say,—

"My dear Kennie, you'll be as good a fisherman as myself yet."

And Kennie would smile, and say he hoped so, for he never meant to be anything else. How little he knew then the truth of the poet's words,—

"There is a Divinity that shapes our ends,
Rough-hew them as we will."

There isn't much fancy work about the flies one needs to catch fish with, on the western shores of Scotland, nor about the rod you use. Only a strongish hook, and tied over that a morsel of white feather or even a bit of wool from the back of a lamb. The fish are not particular when hungry, and they nearly always are hungry, and there are times when you really cannot draw them in fast enough.

But at certain seasons of the year they don't rise; they then prefer bait lowered down to them. They take breakfast in bed. The bait which they love most dearly of all is the inside of a crab, but as this is rather expensive, Kenneth and Duncan Reed were in the habit of using limpets, and they never failed to have good fortune with these.

Of course the limpets had to be gathered first, and as Kenneth was young and Duncan was old, it was the work of the boy to collect these. And when the tide was back you might have seen him at any time, far away out among the weed-covered boulders and rocks, with a chisel and hammer to knock the limpets off and a tiny basket on his back to pop them into.

Nor was there a deal of fancy work to be learned in rowing or sculling a cobble, but then, you know, the fisherman and little Kennie used to venture quite a long distance out to sea, for there was an island three miles away where the fish were very numerous, and thither they often went. And sometimes the sea was both rough and wild before they got back, and skill was then needed to keep her right and straight. For had a sea struck her broadside on, it might have capsized or staved the cobble, and if a great wave had broken over the stern, it might have swamped her, and she would have sunk, and both Kennie and his friend would then have been food for the creatures that dwell down in the dark caves beneath the ocean.

As to swimming, Kenneth seemed to take to it quite naturally, and many a little adventure he had in the water.

Once when swimming he was bitten on the knee by a horrible fish called on the shores of the Atlantic the miller's thumb. It is a kind of skate or ray of immense size, with a fearfully large mouth filled with sharp teeth.

On this particular day the sun had been very bright and the water warm and clear, and Kenneth swam a long distance from the shore. When he returned he was very faint, and his knee was bleeding; he fell and lost consciousness almost immediately after he reached the pebbly beach. Duncan ran to his assistance, and soon got him round; then he bound up his knee.

"Was it a shark?" Kenneth had inquired.

"Oh! horrible! no, Kennie, no, for had a shark seized you, his teeth are so arranged and so hook-like that he couldn't have let you go again had he wanted to ever so much."

"GATHERING THE EGGS OF THE SEA-BIRDS."

Another day, when Duncan and he were hauling in a hand line with an immensely great cod at the end of it, suddenly, for some unexplained reason or other, the line slipped, and almost at the same moment Kenneth fell overboard.

A codfish of say twenty pounds pulls with fearful force.

Kenneth was dragged under the water.

It was a trying time then for old Duncan's nerves. Would the poor boy be dead before he got the great fish checked and in charge again?

Duncan dragged in the line as speedily as he dared.

Oh! how his heart had throbbed to think that there was a possibility of the line breaking, and his little friend being kept under the water till dead.

And oh! how joyful he was when Kenneth reappeared.

Kenneth really came up smiling, though he was spluttering a great deal as well. "I'm sure," he said when he got into the boat again, and the fish was there as well, "I'm sure I've swallowed fully a pint of salt water, Duncan."

Yes, Kenneth laughed heartily about it, but poor old Duncan was weeping, and before he could be himself again he must take off his broad blue bonnet and kneel down upon it in the stern sheets of the cobble, and return thanks to Him who holds the sea in the hollow of His hand.

There were days in summer when the sea was so blue and bright and still, that I think Kenneth used almost to go to sleep while floating on its surface.

Gathering the eggs of the sea-birds from off the cliffs and rocks was dangerous sport, but Kenneth loved it all the more on that account.

But he loved the sea in storm as well, and used to play among the billows and spray along the shore, or venture out a little distance for the pleasure of being rolled up again like a log of wood upon the beach.

Kenneth really could have said with the immortal Byron—

> "And I have loved thee, Ocean! and my joy
> Of youthful sports was on thy breast to be,
> Borne, like thy bubbles, onward; from a boy
> I wantoned with thy breakers—they to me
> Were a delight; and if the freshening sea
> Made them a terror, 'twas a pleasing fear,
> For I was, as it were, a child of thee,
> And trusted to thy billows far and near,
> And laid my hand upon thy mane, as I do here."

Old Duncan Reed owned and worked a little lobster fishery of his own. And before the great grief came that deprived poor Kenneth of a father, he used to take great delight in helping the fisherman with this part of his work. It was very simple. They had wooden cages which they sank at the bottom of a deep pool among the rocks. There was a stone or two at the bottom of each cage to make it sink, and it was lowered down at night by a rope which was attached at the top of the water to a wooden float.

The cages were baited, and Duncan used to find it a capital plan to put a live crab or lobster into the cage. There was a hole at the top of each cage for the creatures to crawl in, but it was so arranged that once in they did not get out again.

As soon as one was sunk, rejoiced to find himself once more in his native element, the imprisoned shell-fish would begin to eat. And presently round would come another crab or lobster and look in for a little at him with his eyes, which, you know, are upon stalks.

"You seem to be enjoying yourself in there," the newcomer would say.

The imprisoned animal would wave a claw at him, as much as to say,—

"Oh! very nicely indeed, but go away; don't stand there and stare at a fellow when he is having his dinner. It is rude."

"Is it good, though?" the other would ask.

"Delicious!" the reply would be.

"How ever did you get inside?"

"Look and see."

Then the new-come lobster would find the hole in the top of the cage, and in he would pop. And presently more and more lobsters would come round and pop in one by one.

Well, but when they wanted to pop out again they would not find it so easy. In fact, there would be no way out for them, until Duncan hauled up the creel and pulled them forth to be boiled.

"It is so easy to get into a trap, but so difficult to get out again," old Duncan would say to Kenneth, "so, my dear laddie, always all your life be sure to look before you leap."

Old Duncan was a very merry old man; he used to tell Kenneth such funny stories, and tales of the deep blue sea, and all about sea-fairies, and water babies, and mermaids that live deep down beneath the ocean in coral caves. I do not think that old Duncan believed in these things himself, nor that he expected Kenneth to believe in them either, but they helped to pass the time, and often of a winter's evening the boy would stay in the fisherman's hut so late that night came on before he started for Glen Alva, and the stars would be all shining as he took his road across the hills and over the dreary moorland where Nancy lived.

Old Duncan Reed did not know the time except by the sun, and Kenneth had no watch, so he could never be sure on occasions like these what o'clock it really was.

But one thing Kenneth never did forget, and that was to bring a few fish or a lobster or a lovely crab for Nancy.

If her light was burning when he reached the little cottage, then he would go in; if not, he knew she had gone to bed, so he would hang the string of fish to the door latch—a very old-fashioned one with a thumb-piece—and go quietly away with Kooran. Or if it was a lobster with its claws tied, he used to tether it to the foot of a rose tree that grew near the door, and poor old Nancy found it in the morning, and was thankful accordingly. I'm sure of this, that Nancy never said her prayers without asking guidance, and a blessing for her bonnie boy.

And it was in this very cottage that Kenneth and Duncan the keeper now found themselves, in front of a nice peat fire, for though it was yet early in autumn, in this bleak Highland moorland the evenings struck chill and cold.

Nancy herself sat in the corner, with her grey grimalkin on her shoulder. The cat seemed asleep, only she had one eye open, and that eye was watching the door.

Chapter Three
The Story of the Fairy Knoll

"I've heard my reverend Grannie say
In lanely glens ye like to stray,
Or where auld ruined castles grey
    Nod to the moon.
Ye fright the nightly wanderer's way,
    Wi' eldritch croon."

Burns.

(Croon—low mournful moan.)

"WINTER, WITH ITS ICY BLASTS."

Scene: The interior of Nancy Dobbell's cottage. Nancy and her visitors round the peat fire, the light from which ever and anon brings the features of each out in bold relief, from the Rembrandtine darkness in the background. Nancy is talking, but knitting as well. Click, click, clickety, click, go the wires, sometimes very fast indeed, at other times more slowly, as if keeping time with Nancy's thoughts and her spoken words.

"And what brings my bairns so late across the muir the nicht?" she asked.

"We knew ye wadna be in bed, Grannie," said Dugald. "The moon is shinin' so brichtly, I had expected to meet ye on the muir, gatherin' herbs by its ghastly licht. We heard the owlet cryin'; had we met you, Grannie, it would have scared our senses awa'."

"I wouldn't have been afraid, Grannie," said Kenneth.

For a moment there was silence, the old woman's head had drooped on her breast, and the knitting wires clicked more slowly, like a clock before it stops.

But only for a moment; she raised her head again, and click, click, click, went the wires as fast as before, but both Kenneth and his companion noticed that Nancy's cheeks were wet.

"Nancy's auld and silly," she said, "but Nancy was not always so. Heigho!"

"Oh, Grannie!" cried honest Dugald, hastening to atone for the cruelty of his first speech, but, in his very hurry, making a poor job of it. "Oh, Grannie, dinna say you're silly; really folk say you're wise and—and—"

"A witch?" said Nancy, smiling.

"Well, may be so. Who can help what people say? But 'deed there is no' a poor woman or man either in a' the glen or parish that hasn't a good word to say for you. Your simple medicines, Grannie, have brought comfort and joy to mony a hoose, no matter where ye got them or who—goodness be near us—helped you to gather them. When puir Jock Kelpie was drooned, did you no' bide and comfort the widow, and sing to her and soothe her for weeks thegither? When Menzies' bairns had the fever, and no' a soul would gang near the hoose, wha tended them and cured them? Wha but Nancy Dobbell? And there's no' a bairn in a' the clachan that doesn't run to meet ye, Grannie, whenever ye come o'er the muir."

The wires clicked very fast.

NANCY DOBBELL'S BIRTHPLACE.

"And," continued Dugald, "though you're maybe no' very bonnie noo, everybody says, 'What a pretty woman Nancy must have been in her time!'"

Nancy's chin fell again, but the wires worked steadily on. Her mind was away back now in the distant past. She was thinking of one summer's evening by Saint Ronan's Well, 'neath the old monk's tree, of a plighted troth and a broken ring, and a lad that went away to sea, and never, never, never came back. A broken ring, and a broken heart, a sorrow that had shadowed her life.

Click, click, click. Ah, well, every life has its romance.

"But Kenneth here has something to tell ye, Grannie."

Clickety, clickety, clickety, go the wires. Nancy is all interest now, for dearly does she love her boy Kennie.

Then Kenneth told her about the fairy knoll and the strange cave he had found in its interior.

He told her all the story, just as we already know it; and for once only during all that evening, the wires ceased to click, and the old woman's hands fell on her lap as she listened.

"It was long, long ago," said Nancy. "Your father, Kennie, was but a boy then, just like you are noo. And his father was but a young man—"

"Ahem!" said the superstitious Highland keeper, giving a hasty half-frightened glance behind him into the darkness. "Ahem! you'll not mak' your story *very* fearsome, will ye, Grannie? Dinna forget the lateness o' the nicht. Mind that we've o'er the lonesome muir to gang yet."

"It was long ago," said Nancy, addressing herself more particularly to Kenneth. "I lived then down by the kirk in the clachan, and there I was born, and the wee village was quieter far in those days than it is even now. Ye know, Kennie, where the burn joins the river, where the old ruin is among the willow trees?"

THE AULD KIRK IN THE CLACHAN.

"Yes, Grannie."

"Well, that house was no ruin then. It was deserted, though. It had gotten a bad name. Nobody would take it; and it seemed falling to pieces. The house stood, as you know, about a mile below your fairy knoll, and two miles beyond is the sea."

"You are right, Grannie."

"Everybody was surprised to find masons and carpenters working at Mill House one morning. It was let. It had been taken by a stranger. Even the laird knew nought about him. Only he paid a year's rent in advance. That was enough for Laird McGee, who was a grippy auld man, and just as rich as grippy.

"It was an ugly house when they made the best of it, two-storied, with red tiles, blintering, blinking windows, and long uncanny-looking attics. It lay a good way back from the road. You went along through a thicket o' willows by a little footpath, then across a stagnant ditch, on a rickety bridge, and this took you to the wild weedy lawn in front of the house itself. Even the road that led past the grounds was little frequented, only a bridle path at best, and it ended at last in a turf dyke (low wall), a march between twa lairds' lands; if you followed this, it took you over the mountains to the seaside village of T—, and the footpath went pretty close to the knoll. A man and woman came to live at Mill House then; they kept a man-servant, and had one child, a pale-faced, old-fashioned-looking hunchback. The man drove a ramshackle trap, so that, taking them altogether, they were no favourites, all the more in that they never put nose beyond the doorstep on the Sabbath day.

"It was always thought, though, that Innkeeper McCaskill, of our clachan, knew more about this family than he cared to tell. Anyhow, he took them all their meat and groceries. And it was noted, too, and remarked upon that he ay took the parcel himsel', a big one it used to be, and the auld grey mare on which he rode was as sorely laden coming as going to Mill House.

"Sometimes, but no' very often, the hunchback laddie used to come on an errand down to the clachan; the bairns o' the village were frightened at him first, frightened even to call him names or throw a sod at him, as bairns will at things that look weird and unco'.

"Corbett was the laddie's name, but the bairns ay ca'd him Corbie.

"Corbie, though, improved on acquaintance. There seemed no harm in him, though, woe is me, he lookit auld, auld-fashioned.

"I suppose Corbie found it lonesome at the Mill House, for whenever he came down to the clachan he tried to mak' acquaintance with the children. It wasna easy to do this. He brought them sweets and wild berries, and bit by bit he won their hearts till Corbie was the greatest favourite in a' the clachan. There was only one house, though, he ever entered, and that was

McCaskill's. But the bairns would meet him on his return, and he ay turned his steps to the auld kirk-yard, and there, on a flat tombstone, he would sit doon and tell them story after story. And a more attentive audience no minister ever had even in the kirk on Sunday. What did Corbie tell them? Oh! just queer auld-world stories he'd heard tell of, or read in books. Stories about witches and warlocks, brownies, sprites, and spunkies. Ay, and about the good folks, the fairies themselves—"

"Dinna, dinna," muttered Dugald. "Think o' the untimous hour, Grannie."

"But one day, as poor Corbie was speakin' and the bairns were listening wi' round eyes and gaping mouths, who should appear on the scene but Corbie's father?

"The laddie gave one low scream, like somebody in a nightmare. Then his father seized him, and oh! they say it was dismal to hear the howls of the poor laddie and the sound o' the fearfu' blows.

"Corbie didn't appear again for many a day, but the human heart must have society, and by degrees Corbie commenced story-telling again, but no' in the kirk-yard, only down in a thicket by the riverside, and always when there, some one was put to watch.

THE OLD MILL HOUSE BY MOONLIGHT.

Kenneth Mcalpine | 33

"I often passed that house, even at night, though the name it had now was worse and worse.

"I had used to have business at T—, across the hills.

"But so bad a name did that road get, that even by day the boldest would hardly venture to take the short cut to T— up along the laird's march dyke. Belated travellers saw lights—dead candles they called them—flitting and flickering around the fairy knoll. Brownies and spunkies, they said, were met on the moor, and down by the riverside Kelpie himsel' was often visible."

(Kelpie, in Scotch folklore a kind of bogle, half man, half bat, often seen by midnight near the banks of ugly rivers. He lives in deep, dark pools.)

"A sturdy shepherd that had stayed too long at T— had met Kelpie, so they said; he was found next day cut and bleeding at the water-side, and was a raving maniac for weeks.

"One day I was setting out for the seaside village—I was young then, and strong—when near the clachan I met McCaskill.

"'Can I trust ye,' he said, 'to deliver a letter at the Mill House?'

"I was feared to offend by refusing, so I took it. But lo! I forgot it a'thegither till I was coming hame. It was night, too, but deliver it I must.

"I took the road alang the auld march dyke across the hills. The moon was shining, but no' very brightly, givin' a feeble yellow kind o' a licht through a haze o' drivin' clouds.

"Well, I was just near the dreariest part o' the upper glen, and no' far from the fairy knoll. I was wishing I were well past it, and away down to the clachan, where I could see the lights blinking cheerily from the houses among the trees.

"I was hurrying on, when suddenly, with an eldritch scream, something in white sprang from behind an etnach," (juniper) "bush.

"I was a bold lass. Some would have fainted. My heart was in my mouth, but I felt impelled to throw myself at the thing, whatever it was. I rushed forward with a frightened shriek and grasped it. I wheeled its face towards the moon, and what think you saw I?"

"A brownie!" said Dugald. "Oh, Grannie, I'm all of a quiver."

"He was no brownie. Only the auld, auld-fashioned face o' little Corbie."

"'Let me go, Nancy. Let me go,' he pleaded. 'My father would kill me if he knew I was found out.'

"He wriggled out o' my hands and fled, and I hardly felt the ground beneath my feet till I reached the low end o' the glen and found myself opposite the gate o' Mill House.

"Then I remembered the letter.

"Dare I deliver it?

"Dare I refuse? That would be worse. I took the road down through the willow thicket, and crossed the rickety auld plank bridge, and in two minutes I was in front of the house. There were sounds of singing and revelry from the inside; I knocked, but wasn't heard. Knocked louder, and in a moment everything was dark and silent. The door opened. I was seized and dragged in. What I saw and heard at Mill House that night I was put on oath not to tell till all were dead or gone. I may tell you now—they were smugglers."

"Thank goodness!" said Dugald, greatly relieved it was no worse. "Oh! Grannie, but you have a fearsome way o' tellin' a story."

"For twa lang years they occupied that house, but during that time something happened that caused grief amang the village bairns. Corbie was missed. Weeks flew by, and he never came back. Then one day a thinly-attended funeral came winding towards the kirk-yard, carrying a wee bit coffin.

"The coffin was Corbie's, and there were many tears and mickle sorrow amang the poor hunchback's acquaintances, I can tell ye. His friends went awa', and left poor Corbie in the mools, but the bairnies ne'er forgot the grave, and mony a bonnie wreath o' buttercups and gowans did they string and put on it in the sweet summer-time.

"Well, laddies, the Mill House was found deserted one day. The smugglers had gone as quietly as they had come. But the house kept its bad name, and so did the hills above it; and so my story ends."

"Not quite," said Dugald. "Did the brownie never come again, or the kelpie? Were the dead candles seen nae mair?"

"No," said Kenneth; "don't you understand? The brownie was the poor boy, Corbie; the kelpie was a smuggler; and the dead candles the lights seen at night near the cave in the fairy knoll. That was the place where they carried on their sinfu' trade."

"I see things clearly enough noo," said Dugald; "and I'll no' be feared to cross the muir. Ah, well, Grannie, you have relieved my mind."

"I'm glad o' it, laddie. Now will Grannie take down the good Book and read a bit?"

Grannie did.

The talk now took a cheerier turn. Old Nancy, knowing how painfully superstitious Dugald was, refrained from introducing anything more in the shape of either brownie or spunkie. And so a pleasant hour was spent, till the old "wag-at-the-wa'" pointed to the hour of twelve, and warned Kenneth and his friend it was high time to commence retracing their steps across the moor.

Chapter Four
Gloaming in the Glen—Kennie's Cave

"Gloaming o'er the glen is falling;
  Little birds have ceased to sing,
Flowerets now their petals faulding
  As night descends on dewy wing."

Anon.

HARVEST IN THE HIGHLANDS.

Scene: Half-way down the glen, where heather and patches of tilled land end, and woodland commences. Where the stream goes wimpling and swirling round the boulders, underneath the rustic bridge.

At the corner, where, after crossing the bridge, the road takes a bend, and is soon lost in the gloom of overhanging foliage, Kenneth is seated on a stone.

At his feet lies Kooran, looking very knowing, because he has got his ears pricked up, and his eyes very wide open, and his head thoughtfully turned a little on one side.

KOORAN.

Kooran knows that his master has come there to meet his friend the Highland keeper, and that the retriever Shot will be with him, but the keeper may come down from the brae-land on the right, or up the road from the wood, or he may suddenly appear on the cliff top, after fording the stream and climbing the rocks.

No need for Kenneth to listen; he has only to watch Kooran.

No sound can deceive Kooran. He will not move from that position till the right moment.

Not far from Kooran's extended tail, a field-mouse begins to sing a little song. She is hidden in under the dry moss, through which she has driven all sorts of smooth round tunnels, for quite an engineer is the field-mouse, and the only wonder is she ever finds her way back again to her nest, through such a labyrinthic network of half-lighted lanes.

"Beet-ee-beet-ee-beet-ee-ee-beet-ee." So goes her song.

38 | Kenneth Mcalpine

Kooran never moves his head; all he does is to turn one ear back towards his tail for a moment, but *only* one ear.

"I hear you," he seems to say. "Sing away, my pretty one you know I'm busy, but wait a wee till Shot comes. Shot and I will soon have you out of there. My eyes! won't we make the turf fly!"

A great bird flies right over a tree, but turns sharply in the air and flies back affrightedly. It was a moor-cock, but he didn't know any one was there. He has to take another road home.

A twig snaps; Kenneth looks in that direction. The dog never moves. He knows it is only the polecat trying to reach out to a branch where a thrush has gone to sleep.

The stream makes music in drowsy monotone, but hark! there is a plash. It is an otter. Kooran knows it, and does not move. Then presently there are close beside them apparently, two sharp dull thuds. It is only mother rabbit beating her heels on the ground to drive her over-bold little ones back into their holes, and to warn every rabbit within hearing that danger is near, and that there are a live dog and a live boy not far off, who can't be after any good.

"DANGER IS NEAR."

Sometimes the distant bleating of sheep or the pleasant lowing of kine falls on Kenneth's ear, and anon, far up among the mountains, there is a strange shout, half whoop, half whistle, prolonged and mournful. At first it is repeated about every two seconds; then Quicker and quicker it comes, and wilder and wilder, till it ends in one long quavering scream.

"Whoo-oop, whoo-oop, whoo-oop, whoop, whoop-oop-oop-oop-oo-oo-oo!"

It is the shriek of the curlew as he sails round and round in the air.

"Why, Kooran," says the boy at last, "what can be keeping them?"

Kooran beats his tail twice on the ground, but does not move his body.

"I hope they won't be long, dear doggie."

Kooran beats his tail once against the ground.

This means, "Have patience, master."

The sun goes down behind the hills.

Then comes still Evening on.

In the bonnie Scottish Highlands, reader, in sweet summer-time, or in riper autumn, we cannot say with truth that night falls; no, rather "Evening steals down."

Oh! how gently she is stealing down now on the peaceful scene around Kenneth and Kooran. Far down the glen yonder, where the river broadens out in the valley, there lie long clouds of grey mist, with the tall spruce pines glimmering green and ghost-like through them. They are the trailing garments of Evening. Gradually they change to crimson as the sun's parting rays fall on them.

But day lingers long on the hill-tops, among the steel-grey rocks, among boulders that stand boldly out from the dark background like blocks of snow, and among patches of purple heather. Evening sees that day must go at last, so she hies away to put the flowers to sleep.

"Sleep, sleep, my gentle flowers," she says, "for the day is dying fast, and the dews will fall and blight you."

She whispers to the gowans (mountain daisies) first, and the "wee modest crimson-tippèd flowers" fold their petals like sea-anemones, and go softly to sleep. She lightly touches the pimpernels, the crimson and the pink-eyed, and they curl their flower-leaves and sink to rest. She breathes upon the wild convolvulus that trails among the grass, and it twists up its silken blossoms till they look like little wisps of calico, pink and white. Even the hardy heather bells creep closer together, and the star-like blossoms of the bramble that clothe the banks shrink smaller as she brushes them with her wings.

"THEN CAME STILL EVENING ON."

Then Evening speaks to the west wind.

"Blow softly, gentle west wind," she says; "blow softly through the feathery larches and the needled pines; make the leaves of the russet oaks and the silvery drooping birches sing soft lullabies, that my children the flowers may sleep."

And the west wind obeys her, and goes sighing through the trees, and all the flowerets nod and sleep.

The linnet has long gone to bed, close hidden under the whin bush. The tom-tit creeps closer against a patch of lichen that grows on the stem of an old ash tree. The cushat in the thicket of spruce hears the west wind's lullaby, and ceases to croodle. The blackbird and thrush hide themselves in the hawthorn tree; only the robin still sings on the top rail of the old bridge.

"I will sing all night," the robin says. "I will sing with the trees and the west wind till the sun returns."

"Twhoo-hoo-hoo!" shrieks the owl, and Robin flies away.

Then Evening goes to the hedgehog, to the fox, to the foumart, the whitterit, the bat, and the vole.

"Come out now, come out now," she cries to these, "for the moon is coming, and danger has fled with the daylight far over the hills."

But the lithe green snake, and the deadly adder, and the toad have heard the invitation too, and lie closer under cover or creep into their holes, for enemies are abroad.

Then slowly and solemnly over the distant hills uprises the moon.

And so gloaming gives place to night.

Something black came feathering along at last, and next moment Shot, with his jacket quite wet, and very much out of breath with running, was kissing his friend the collie.

Very soon after Dugald and Kenneth were shaking hands.

"You thought I wasn't coming?" said Dugald.

"Indeed, you're right, but I had almost fallen asleep."

"I've had such a chase after a couple of poachers. Didn't you hear me firing? No? But troth, I did have a rap at one of them. Didn't kill him? Man, no, and more's the pity. Troth, Kennie, lad, there are too many about. But come along, till we see the fairy's knoll. Man, it's a whole week since I've seen you. How's the sheep?"

"Doing well. No more late lambs. No more feeble dying ones."

The keeper shouldered his gun; the two dogs speedily tore up the grass where the field-mouse had been singing. They destroyed all her tunnels and mossy lanes, but they hadn't time to unearth the mouse herself.

Away up over the hills went the friends. Up, and up, and up. When on the brow of the mountain they were to cross they must have been fifteen hundred feet above the sea level. Down beneath them the rolling country was slumbering in the misty moonlight, only the river meandered through it all and sparkled like a thread of silver.

It was a near cut they had taken; they had now only to descend a little way, and, behold, they were at the cave.

And soon in it.

"I'll light the lamp," said Kenneth, and in a moment more the interior was illuminated.

"Well, I do declare this is grand! Never in this world before had shepherd such a shelter, surely!"

So he well might say. Kenneth had cleaned the cave out, bedded the floor with a carpet of withered brackens, hung a huge oil lamp in it, which gave light and warmth both, built rude seats round it, made a rude table, and conveyed hither his books, his fishing-gear, and even his flute.

"Isn't it delightful!" cried Kenneth, laughing till his eyes danced and sparkled in the moonlight.

"Oh! it is grand!" said Dugald, sitting down all the better to view the place.

"I can eat my dinner here, you know," said Kenneth, "and read my books, and study at night."

"At night!" exclaimed honest Dugald. "Wad ye no' be feared, man?" he added solemnly. "Are there no bogles about? Losh! there might be even ghosts. Or, man! just fancy a wee fairy body coming in through the door when you were a' by yoursel'!"

"Oh!" cried the boy, "that is too good ever to be true. I should rejoice to see a fairy."

"Well, man, rather you than me. But tak' your flute and play a tune, to banish eerie thoughts."

Kenneth put his instrument together and commenced.

Shot sat down on the brackens and commenced too.

Dugald turned Shot out of the cave, but Kooran had better manners and was allowed to stay. It was the "Flowers o' the Forest" that Kenneth played, and to this sweetly mournful air Dugald listened entranced.

"Silly Dugald!" some would say, for his very eyes were moist.

"Ah! Kennie, man," he said at last, "I hope you may never live to play that dear auld lilt in a foreign land with the tears rinnin' o'er your face."

"What mean ye, Dugald?" Kenneth said.

"Mean?" cried Dugald almost fiercely. "Why, this, lad: that news came to-day to the clachan that our auld laird, that has ever been sae kind to us, is bankrupt, and has sold his fine estate to an American—to a foreigner, Kennie."

"Don't say so?"

"But I do say so, and I fear it's an owertrue tale, lad. The place that knows us noo may soon know us no more. For they tell me he is going to evict the tenants, pull the clachan down, and turn our bonnie glen into a forest for deer, knock doon the dear auld kirk, Kennie, that you and I were christened in, and have sung psalms in Sunday after Sunday, knock doon our kirk, give our roofs to the flames,—ay, Kennie, and level the graves o' those we hold dear!"

"I really cannot believe all this, Dugald. Oh! it would kill my mother."

"Poor laddie!" said Dugald, laying his hand kindly on Kenneth's shoulder. "Poor laddie! Grief has been your share in the world of late. Two or three years ago, when your father lived, what a merry boy you were! But your father, once a thrifty crofter, had been reduced to a humble shepherd, and when that broke his heart, and the Lord took him, his brave boy Kennie left school and tended the sheep, and his industry supports a widowed mother. Ay, lad, Kennie, it will gang hard on you and hard on your mother to leave Glen Alva."

Kenneth looked the picture of despair. His flute had fallen from his hand, and lay unheeded among the brackens.

"To leave my mother," he muttered, speaking apparently to himself, "to go into a foreign land, that were bad, but to know that the very glen itself was altered, the old kirk roofless, the houses heaps of ruins, to have nothing to look back to, nothing at home to love—oh! Duncan, Duncan, that wouldn't be absence from home; it would be banishment, Duncan, banishment and exile."

"Let us try no' to think about it, Kennie. Dinna look so woe-begone, man, or you'll mak' me sorry that I've told you."

The boy turned quickly round.

"Oh! but say you've been but joking. Say it is not true, Duncan."

"Oh hey!" was Duncan's answer—a big sigh, that was all.

"But you know," said Duncan, after a pause, "nobody is sure yet of anything."

The boy laughed now.

"Ha! ha! yes," he cried, tearing himself away from gloomy thoughts. "We'll have hope. We won't think about it, will we? Ha! ha! no, we won't think about it. And I'll never say a single word to my mother about the matter. It *may* pass, you know.

"And so," he continued, "you really like my cave. Well, little Archie, your son, will often be here with me. And you must come too, and we'll have such fun. I wonder if the ptarmigans will build next year in the same place as they did last. Mind when the snow falls you'll take me for a day's white hare hunting, won't you? It is such grand sport, and you promised, you know. What tune did you say I was to play? Something merry. Oh! yes, I know—"

Kenneth recovered his flute from among the brackens as he spoke, and rattled off into as merry a reel as ever witches danced to in "Alloway's auld haunted kirk."

"First-rate!" cried Duncan, clapping his hands, while even Kooran barked for joy, and Shot's voice gave gladsome echo at the cave's mouth. "First-rate! man; that's the kind o' music to banish the bogies. Losh! Kennie, music like that would have made Methuselah himsel' grow young again. That it would."

It was late that evening ere the two friends found themselves down the glen again, but when they bade each other good-night and walked briskly homewards there was not a thought in their hearts of evil to come; they were each as happy as the lark that carols o'er spring corn.

Chapter Five
A Day in the Wilds

"My heather land, my heather land,
Though fairer lands there be,
Thy gowany braes in early days
Were gowden ways to me."

Thom.

Scene: The fairy's glen high up among the mountains. Kenneth seated, book in hand, on the top of the fairy knoll, which stands out strangely green against the purples and browns which surround it. Kenneth is alone. Kooran is away down beneath, minding the sheep. The shepherd-boy lays down the book at last, or rather he drops it down the chimney of his cave, and it falls on the carpet of brackens beneath. Then he takes his crook, and goes slowly down the strath.

This was a Saturday forenoon, and Kenneth and his little friend Archie McCrane were going on a long round of pleasure.

Ha! yonder comes Archie. Or rather, yonder suddenly doth he appear. He comes straight up out of the centre of a bush of furze, in quite a startling kind of way.

Archie is eleven years of age, though very tiny, but very strong, and as hard as an Arab. No fat about Archie. His face and bare neck and breast and thorn-scratched knees are as red as if recently rubbed with brick-dust. There isn't a rent or hole in either his jacket or kilt, but woe is me, it is pretty nearly all patches; it is mother's work every night to mend the rents Archie makes in his clothes. Archie is, of course, his mother's darling. She even takes pains to make him pretty. She prides herself even in his beautiful hair. His hair is one of Archie's strong points. Mind, he wears no bonnet (cap), never did and never would. He owns one, but always forgets to put it on. So his soft golden hair is cut across above the brows, and hangs in wavy luxuriance over his shoulders. I said golden, but it is more straw colour, and bleached on the top almost white.

He is a singular lad, Archie, has a half-wild, half-frightened look in his face; in fact, take him all in all, he is quite in keeping with the romantic surroundings.

"I've got him," Archie said.

"What is it?"

"A little black rabbit."

"Strange," said Kenneth; "put him down. He must be half tame, I should think."

Archie put it down, and the two boys knelt beside it among the heather. It was a half-grown one, so mild, so gentle-looking. Butter, you would have said, wouldn't melt in that wee rabbit's mouth. And it crouched down low and held its ears flat against its back, and never moved an eye or winked, but allowed the lads to smooth it with their fore-fingers.

But all at once, pop! it was off like an eel.

"Oh?" said Archie, with such a disappointed look, "and I meant to take it hame wi' me."

Kenneth laughed, and off the two scampered, as wild as any rabbits.

"Shot is here," said Archie.

"Where?"

"Down with Kooran."

"Then you must whistle him up; Kooran will look after the sheep by himself, but Shot will lead him into temptation. Besides, the sheep don't know Shot. Whistle, Archie, whistle, man."

Archie put four fingers in his mouth and emitted a scream as shrill as the scream of the great whaup. (The curlew.) In a moment more Shot was coming tearing along through the heather.

And with him was Kooran.

"What do you want, Kooran?"

Kooran threw himself in a pleading attitude at his master's feet, looked up with brown, melting, pleading eyes, and wagged his tail.

"Oh! I know, dear doggie," said Kenneth; "you want your dinner, because you know we'll be away all day."

Kooran jumped and capered and danced and barked, and Kenneth rolled a piece of cake and a bit of cheese in a morsel of paper and handed it to the dog.

"Keep the koorichan," (sheep) "well together, doggie," he said; "and don't take your dinner for an hour yet."

Kooran gave his tail a few farewell wags and galloped off, but as soon as he was in sight of the flock and out of sight of his master, he lay down and ate his dinner right up at once. He ate the cheese first, because it smelt so nice, and then he ate the cake.

Away went Archie and Kenneth and Shot. It didn't take them long to gallop through the heather and furze. Of course the furze made their bare knees bleed, but they did not mind that.

LEFT IN CHARGE.

They reached the road in twenty minutes, and went straight away to the clachan to report themselves at the manse, or minister's house.

It wasn't much of a manse, only an ordinary-looking, blue-slated house of two stories, but it had a nice lawn in front and gardens round it, where ash trees, limes, planes, and elms grew almost in too great abundance. The windows were large, and one was a French one, and opened under a verandah on to the lawn. This was the Rev. David Grant's study.

Before they came round the hedgerow, both boys stopped, dipped their handkerchiefs in the running brook, and polished their faces; then they warned Shot to be on his best behaviour, and looking as sedate and solemn as they could, they opened the gate, and made their way to the hall door. And Shot tried to look as old as he could, and followed behind with his nose pretty near the ground, and his tail almost between his heels.

But Mr Grant himself saw them, opened the casement window, and cried,—

"Come this way, boys."

Mr Grant was the clergyman of the village. The living was a poor one, and as he had seven grown-up daughters, he was obliged to turn sheep farmer. It was his sheep that Kenneth herded, and that his father had herded before him, after "the bad years" had ruined the poor man.

"Miss Grant will soon be here," he said. "And how have you left the sheep, Kenneth?"

"They are all nicely, thank you, sir," replied Kenneth.

"All healthy and thriving, I hope?"

"Oh, yes, sir, we won't have any more trouble, and Kooran is minding them. He will take capital care of them, sir. And Duncan McCrane, Archie's father, is going up himself to see them."

"That's right," said Mr Grant.

The Misses Grant were the mothers of the clachan. I haven't space to tell you half of the good they did, so I shall not attempt it, but they taught in school and Sunday-school, they knew all the deserving poor, and attended them when sick, and advised them, and prayed with them, and read to them, and never went empty-handed to see them. Why, they even begged for them. And they knew the undeserving poor, and did good to them also. Even Gillespie, the most dreaded poacher and wildest man in the clachan, was softened in tone and like a child when talking to the "good Miss Grants," as they were always called.

Well, every one loved these homely sisterly lassies of the parson's.

"By-the-bye, Kennie," said Mr Grant, "I hear the glen is going to be evicted."

"Surely, sir, that isn't true?" replied Kenneth.

Miss Grant the elder was Kenneth's teacher, one of them, old Nancy Dobbell was another, and Nature was a third.

"Did you come for a lesson to-day?" said Miss Grant, entering.

"No, thank you. Miss Grant."

"Well, I'm glad, because I was going out. Little Miss Redmond is here with her governess. They have the pony trap, and I am going to their glen with them to lunch. Come to the drawing-room; they are there."

Miss Redmond was the only daughter of an Englishman of wealth, who had bought land in an adjoining glen. Mr Redmond himself was seldom at home—if, indeed, Scotland could be called his home—and his wife was an invalid.

But there was nothing of the invalid about little Jessie, the daughter. Quite a child she was, hardly more than eight, but with all the quiet dignity and easy affability that is only to be found among children of the *bon ton*.

Archie was simply afraid of her. Kenneth got on better, however. He answered all her innocent but pointed questions, as if he were talking to his grandmother. But Jessie was really asking for information, and Kenneth knew it, so the two had quite a serious old-fashioned conversation.

Well, Kenneth seemed a gentleman born. He sat easily in his chair, he held his cap easily, and behaved himself with polite *sang froid*. Miss Grant was proud of Kenneth.

But poor Archie looked ill at ease.

Kenneth told Jessie the story of the little black rabbit, and Jessie was much interested.

"What did it look like?" she asked.

Kenneth glanced towards Archie.

"He just looked," he answered, "as Archie is looking now, as if waiting a chance to bolt."

This was a very mischievous speech, but Kenneth could not refrain from saying what he thought.

"Poor boy?" said Jessie, as if she had been Archie's mother; "he appears to be very frightened. What beautiful hair he has! It is just like mine."

This was true, only Jesssie's was longer and not bleached. Kenneth sat looking half wonderingly at Jessie, longer than politeness would dictate.

"What are you thinking about?" said Jessie.

"I was thinking," said Kenneth, candidly, "I'd give all the world to be able to talk English in the pretty way you do."

"Some day," Jessie said to her governess, "we will go and see the sheep, Miss Gale. Remember that place. Put it down in your notes. We are to see a fairy knoll and a smugglers' cave. It will be so delightful."

"We go to London soon for the winter," said Miss Gale, "but will come and see you, Kenneth, in spring or summer."

"Miss Gale," insisted the imperious Jessie, "I haven't seen you use your tablets."

So Miss Gale smilingly took her tablets out and noted the engagement to visit the sheep and see the fairy knoll.

"He has a flute," said Archie, with sudden determination not to sit mute all the time; "make him play."

And Kenneth had to play, just the same old melodies that the Scotch so dearly love; but as he played there came so sweet and sad an expression into English Jessie's face, that Kenneth would have played for hours to please her.

When he had done, she went and looked at Miss Gale's tablets.

"Thank you," she said, "dear Miss Gale, but just under there write, 'Flute.'"

So the word "Flute" was added. It was something for the child to think about while in London, a treat to look forward to, a long summer's day to be spent among the heather, among the sheep, a fairy glen, a real fairy knoll, and dreamy music from a flute.

No sooner was Archie round the corner of the hedge and out of sight of the parson's window, than he gave a wild whoop, like an Apache Indian, and ran off.

Kenneth came up with him before long. Not quite up with him, though, because Archie was high, high up in the sky, at an old magpie's nest. The magpie was done with it, and Archie was tearing it down.

"The nasty old chick-chicking thing!" he explained to Kenneth; "for two years running she has used the same old nest, and it wasna hers to begin wi', but a hoody-craw's."

Away went the boys together. They had a long day before them, and meant to make use of it. They were as happy as boys could be who could do as they pleased and go where they pleased, and had bread and cheese to eat when hungry.

Very practical naturalists were Kenneth and Archie. They knew nothing whatever of nomenclature, they could not have told you the Latin name of any of the hundred and one strange wild creatures they met every day in their wanderings over mountain and moorland, but about the habits of those creatures there was nothing they could not have told you.

They could have led you to the home of the red deer and moor-cock. They knew the tricks and the manners of every bird that built in hedgerow or furze bush, in thicket of spruce or pine-top or larch, in the hay or the heather or the growing corn, among sedges by the sides of lonely lochs or tarns, in banks or holes by the side of the stream, in hillock or stony cairn, or far up the mountain's side almost at the snow line itself.

They knew every bird by its name (in Scotch), by its eggs, by its nest, either in shape or in lining, and they knew where to look for every nest.

Remember this, and I'm proud to mention it, these boys never destroyed a nest nor an egg.

They knew all about animals that couldn't fly also, and oh! their name is legion. They knew or could pretty well guess, when they came across any of these, what the particular little animal, whether field-mouse, squirrel, polecat, or vole, was about, and what it was after, whether food for the young at home, or a warm bit of moss for extra comfort in the nest, or twigs, rushes, dry weeds, or hay for building purposes.

There was no deceiving Kenneth or Archie, nor Kooran and Shot, for the matter of that. But the wild creatures knew the boys, and often objected to have their nests examined, and even tried to deceive them.

For example, the hedgehog one evening in the gloaming was caught in the very act of hauling away an immensely long earthworm. The hoggie didn't curl up, but sat down and made pretence to eat it. But Archie knew the nest was not far away.

The fox had a home in the middle of the pine wood and had young there, and do what she would, the old mother fox could not get the puppies to keep to the hole and lie in bed all day. They would come out and play and tumble in the clearing, in such a funny ridiculous way. Once Archie was coming up towards this clearing, and the puppies were all out, for father fox was from home looking after chickens, and as soon as mother fox carried one into the hole in her mouth and went back for another, it came laughing and frolicking out again. So half distracted the mother went slily to meet Archie, and pretended she was nearly dead, and went away in a different direction from the clearing, and dragged one leg behind her in a way that made Archie certain he could catch her. Of course when mother fox had Archie far enough away she disappeared. But Archie came back next night, and the same trick did not succeed again, so he found the puppy foxes and used to play with them for hours at a time in the clearing.

The lapwings have a trick in spring-time of pretending they have a broken wing when you go near the nest. They fall down in front of you, and pretend they can't get away fast, and you run to catch them and forget all about the nest. This is a very clever trick, and has deceived many, but Archie used to shake his yellow hair and laugh at the lapwing.

"It is too thin," Archie would say. "I'm not a town's boy."

And he would go straight away and find the nest, with the buff and black speckled eggs, on the top of the bare sunny hillock where in a hole— not worth the name of nest—lappie had laid them.

It was too late in the season now to look for birds' nests, but they saw to-day a lot of old nests that they had not found the summer before, for the trees were now getting bare and thin in foliage.

When tired roaming about in the wilds, the two boys sat down and had dinner.

Then they crossed the wide moorland to Nancy's lonely cottage.

Nancy was delighted to see them. She said they must be hungry. But the boys assured her that they were not, because they had had plenty of bread and cheese. But Nancy put down her knitting and warmed some heather ale for them, and sweetened it, and switched two new-laid eggs, and mixed those in it, and made the boys drink the harmless and delicious beverage.

Then she took up her knitting again, and click, click, clickety-click, went the wires the while she told them strange old-world stories and tales of fairies and kelpies.

The boys were entranced, and it was nearly dark when they left Nancy's cottage and betook themselves to the glen. Kooran was very pleased to see them back, and helped them to fold the sheep; then the whole four—that is, Kenneth and Archie and Kooran and Shot—went up the fairy glen to the fairy knoll and the smugglers' cave.

Kenneth lit the lamp; then he lit a fire out of doors and hung over a pot from a tripod, quite gipsy fashion.

Kenneth was a capital cook, and made a rabbit stew that a king might have eaten. So both boys supped royally, and the dogs had the bones.

Then the things were cleared away, and down lay Archie on the dais, to listen to Kenneth reading the "Tales of the Borders."

On the whole, they had spent a most delightful day of it. But it was only one of many, for Saturday was Kenneth's own day, and Archie was his constant companion.

And so the autumn wore away among these, peaceful glens. The days grew shorter and shorter, the frosts fell morning and night, and winds moaned through trees leafless and bare. The sheep were folded now in fields on the lower lands, and Kenneth had more time for his studies. But every evening found Archie and him in their cave in the fairy knoll.

Chapter Six
Kenneth

Scene: Glen Alva in a winter garb. A morning in December. A glorious morning and yet how great a change from the day before. For on the west coast of Scotland changes do come soon and sudden.

Last night, ere gloaming fell, Kenneth had stood at his mother's cottage door for hours watching the sunset and the weird but splendid after-glow.

The sun had gone down rosy red and large behind a grey-blue bank of rock-and-tower clouds that bounded the horizon above the hills. But so strange and beautiful was the colour that soon spread over the firmament, with its tints of lavender, yellow, pink, and pale sea-green, that even Kenneth's mother must hold up her hands and cry,—

"Oh! dear laddie, a sky like that, I fear, bodes no good to the glen."

For uppermost in every one's mind in Glen Alva, at the present time, was the threatened eviction.

Then, just one hour afterwards, the pink colour had disappeared from the sky, and the yellow had changed to one of the reddest, fieriest orange hues ever eyes had looked upon; while away farther round towards the north the sky was an ocean of darkest green. The trees, ashes and elms, that bordered a field adjoining the kail-yard, stood strangely out against this glow; every branchlet and twig seemed traced in ink—the blackest of the black.

Above this orange, or rather through its upper edge, where it went melting into the zenith's blue, the stars glimmered green.

But looking earthward, all around the hills and fields were dark and bare, for winter had not yet donned her mantle of snow.

And now Kenneth has come out of doors almost before the sun is risen, for there are fowls to be fed, and rabbits and guinea-pigs, and the cow herself to be seen to, before he takes his own breakfast and starts to meet Dugald to enjoy a day among the hills.

What a change! The hoar frost has been falling gently all the livelong night. The good fairies seem to have been at work while others slept, changing the world to what he now sees it, and so silently too. And this is what strikes Kenneth as so wonderful: while shrub, and tree, and weeds, and grass, and heather, are transformed, as it were, into powdered ice, there is neither loss of shape nor form; not a branch bends down; not a leaf or twig is out of place. And the very commonest of objects, too, are turned to marvels of beauty.

The trees point heavenwards with fingers of coral. But to look lower down. Surely there could be no romance or beauty about a cabbage leaf. Glance at these then fringed all round with needles and spiculae inches long; the leaf itself is a shimmering green, dusted over with a frosty down. The wire-netting around the poultry run, and the cobwebs that depend from outhouse eaves, are shiny silver lace-work all. A glorious morning, a wondrous scene; why, even the humble clothes line is changed into a white and feathery cable, and the tufts of grass that grow on the pathways are tufts of grass no longer, but radiant bunches of snow-white feathers.

Adown the glen, where Kenneth wanders at last, everything around him is of the same magical beauty, a beauty that is increased tenfold when he reaches the woods. Here, too, all is silence, only the murmur of the rippling stream, or the peevish twitter of birds, or the complaining notes of a throstle as she flies outwards from a thicket, scattering the silvery powder all around her.

But down here in the wood, through the dazzling white of the pine trees, the cypresses, and spruces and holly, comes a shade, a shimmer of green, brighter among the pines themselves, darker among the ivy that clings to their stems. And the seed balls on the ivy itself are globes of feathery snow, and every spine on the holly leaves is a fairy plume.

Hark! the sound of ringing footsteps on frost-hard road, and a manly merry voice singing,—

> "Cam' ye by Athol, lad wi' the philibeg,
> Down by the Tummel and banks o' the Garry?
> Saw ye the lad wi' his bonnet and white cockade,
> Leaving his mountains to follow Prince Charlie?"

ARCHIE'S COTTAGE.

—And next moment, gun on shoulder, sturdy Dugald the keeper stalks round the corner.

"The top of the mornin' to ye, man," said Dugald. "Have you seen Archie?"

"No, not yet."

But even as they spoke Archie, bare-headed as usual, is seen coming up from the side of the stream, with a string of beautiful mountain trout in his hand.

He climbed up through the icy ferns, leapt the fence, and stood before them.

"I set twenty lines last night," he said, in joyful accents, "and caught thirteen trout."

Back the trio went to Mrs McAlpine's cottage, and those fish were fried for breakfast, with nut-brown tea, cream, and butter and cakes; and if there be anything in this world better for breakfast than mountain trout fresh from a stream, I trust some kind soul will send me a hamper of it.

What a day of it they had among the hills, to be sure!

Young as he was, Kenneth had a gun, while Archie did duty as ghillie; they went miles and miles away up among the mountains where the heather grew high as their waists—Kenneth's waist and Dugald's, I mean; it was often over Archie's head. But they came out of this darkness at last, and shook the snow off their jackets and kilts, and walked on over the moorland.

Gorcocks stretched their red necks and stared at them in wonder. Ptarmigans, too cold to fly, ran and hid in the heather, the black cock and the grey hen often flew past them with a wild whirr-r-r, while far above, circling round and round in the blue sunny sky, was the bird of Jove himself.

But it was not the gorcock, nor black cock, nor the ptarmigan, nor the great golden eagle itself they were after, but the white or mountain hare.

And the sport was good. They took time to dine, though, for the air was bracing and keen; then they shot again till nearly sunset, and Kenneth's cheek flushed redder than usual as Dugald praised him for his skill as a marksman. But at the same time Dugald praised himself indirectly, for he added, "But no thanks to you, lad; sure, haven't you had Dugald McCrane himself to teach you this many a long day?"

Archie was wonderfully strong, but he couldn't carry half the hares, so Dugald and Kenneth had to help him as well as carry their own and their guns, and even Shot carried a white hare all the way to the glen below.

"Of course," said Kenneth, "you'll come up the glen, Dugald, to our cottage, and let us show my mother our game; she will be so pleased."

"'Deed, and I will, then," replied Dugald, "and there will be a pair of hares for the old lady, too, and one for Nancy the witch—goodness be about us—for the laird wrote me to say if I killed more than a dozen and a half today, I was to do what I liked with the rest."

"Dear old laird!" said Kenneth; "why doesn't he come down from London and stay among his people? We all love him so much."

"Ah! Kennie, he has ruined himself, like mony mair Highland lairds, by stoppin' in the big city, and it's myself that is sorry. But see, wha comes here?"

It was a tall stranger, dressed in knickerbockers, a broad-brimmed soft felt hat, and a surtout coat, a very ridiculous association of garments.

He carried a gun over his shoulder, and two beautiful Irish setters walked behind him. Both dogs were lame.

"Hullo, fellows!" he said. "Glad I've met some one at last. How far have I to walk to the little inn at the klakkin?"

Dugald threw down his game-bag, so did the others their burdens. No one was sorry to rest a bit, so they leant against the dyke and quietly surveyed the stranger. Meanwhile Shot was standing defiantly in front of the setters.

Shot wanted to know if either of these dogs would oblige him by fighting, singly or the two at once. But they did not seem inclined to accept the challenge.

"My good fellow," said the stranger, "when you have stared sufficiently to satisfy you, perhaps you will be good enough to answer my question."

"Well," said Dugald, "I'm staring because it's astonished I am."

"You'd be more astonished if you knew who I am. But never mind. I've been travelling all day among these tiresome hills and only managed to kill one brown hare. I was told at the inn that the white hares were in hundreds."

"Very likely," said Dugald, "but it's no' in the glen you'll find them."

"You're two miles from the clachan," continued Dugald. "I'm McGregor's keeper—his chief keeper. I'll trouble you, sir, to show your permit."

"You're a saucy fellow. I'm the future owner of these glens and all the estate, and lord of Castle Alva."

"I'll believe it when I see it. You're neither lord nor laird yet. Your permit, please. I believe nobody since two students poached all over the hills here and called themselves friends of the laird's."

"As to my permit, fellow, I did not trouble to bring it from C—."

"Then you'll consider yourself my prisoner till you can produce it."

The stranger was a man about forty-five, tall and wiry and haughty. He looked at Dugald up and down for a moment.

"Dare you, fellow?" he shouted.

Dugald quietly laid down his gun and threw off his jacket. He then took off his scarf, and stretched it out in front of the stranger. It measured fully a yard and a half.

"I've tied the hands and feet of a poacher before," he said, "a bigger man than you. And I mean to do my duty by you."

"Dugald," said Kenneth, "this gentleman may really be what he says."

"Let him come quietly, then," replied Dugald. "No stranger that ever walked will lead Dugald McCrane into trouble again. Is it going to surrender you are, sir? Consider while I count ten. One—two—three—"

"Enough, enough. I'm your prisoner, fellow. It is very ridiculous. Perhaps you'll live to rue this day. Come on with me to the inn."

Dugald laughed.

"Not just yet," he answered; "it's the other way; you come with me."

The stranger bit his lip and frowned.

Then he put his hand in his pocket and produced a gold piece.

"This is yours," he said, "if you come at once."

Fire seemed to flash from Dugald's eyes. He clenched his fists convulsively, and looked for a moment as if he meant to spring at the stranger's neck.

"Put up your bawbees," he said at length. "If Highlanders are poor, they are also proud, and the gold isn't dug yet that would tempt Dugald McCrane to neglect his duty. And if the auld laird himsel' was standing there, he'd tell you it's the truth I'm speaking. Right about face, my man, and march with us to the glen-head, or it may be the worse for you."

The stranger gave a sigh and a sickly kind of smile, but he shouldered his gun and prepared to follow.

"One minute," said Dugald, for Kenneth had beckoned him aside.

Kenneth and he conversed for a moment; then Dugald returned.

"You look tired," he said, shortly; "we'll go your road. Archie," he continued, "pick the ice-balls from the feet of those twa poor dogs. Your dogs, sir, are but little used to our Hielan' hills."

"And indeed, my fine fellow," replied the stranger, "am but little used to your Highland manners, but grateful to you, young sir,"—he was addressing Kenneth—"for saving me a longer journey than needful."

In half an hour's time the future laird of Alva, for it was no other, found himself a prisoner at the little inn of the clachan. This for a night; next day he produced a letter from McGregor himself—he had despatched a messenger to C— for it—which quite satisfied Dugald McCrane.

Dugald was satisfied of something else as well, namely, that he had done his duty without exceeding it.

Kenneth and Dugald visited Nancy Dobbell's next day and told her the story.

"Och! och!" she said, "it will be a sore day for the folks of the clachan, when a stranger steps into the shoes of poor auld Laird McGregor.

"But a cloud is rising o'er the hills, my laddies; there will be little more peace in Glen Alva. A cloud is rising o'er the hills, and that cloud will burst, and wreck and ruin will fall on the poor people. My dreams have told me this many and many a day since. Heigho! but Nancy's time is wearin' through. She'll never live to see it."

Kenneth took the old thin hand that lay in her lap in both his, and looked into her face, while the tears gathered in his eyes.

He was going to say something. But he did not dare trust himself to speak. He simply petted the poor wrinkled hand.

Is Campbell the poet right, I wonder?

> "*Does* the sunset of life give us mystical lore?
> *Do* coming events cast their shadows before?"

Chapter Seven
The Death of Poor Nancy

"I'm wearin' awa', Jean,
Like snaw-wreaths in thaw, Jean;
I'm wearin' awa'
To the Land o' the Leal."

Old Song.

Scene: Kenneth at home in his mother's humble cot. A fire of peats and wood burning on the low hearth. Kenneth's mother reading the good Book with spectacles on her eyes. Kenneth leading also at the other side of the fire. Above the mantelpiece a black iron oil lamp is burning, with old-fashioned wicks made from peeled and dried rushes. Between the pair, his head on his paws, Kooran is lying. He is asleep, and probably dreaming of the sheep that he cannot get to enter the "fauld," for he is emitting little sharp cheeping barks, as dogs often do when they dream.

Kenneth gets up at last and reaches down his plaid and crook.

"Dear laddie," says his mother, "you're surely not going out to-night!"

Kooran jumps up and shakes himself.

"Yes, mother; I must," is the quiet reply. "I had a strange dream about poor Nancy last night. She has been ill, you know, and I haven't called for three days."

"But in such a night, laddie! Listen to the wind! Hear how the snow and the hail are beating on the window!"

Kenneth did listen.

It was indeed a fearful night.

The wind was sighing and crying through every cranny of the window, and shaking the sash; it was howling round the chimney, and wailing through the keyhole of the door.

Snow was sifting in underneath the door, too, and lying along the floor like a stripe of light.

Kenneth drew his plaid closer round him.

"I must go, mother," he said; "I could not sleep to-night if I didn't."

"Don't be uneasy about me even if I don't return till morning. I may stay all night at Dugald's."

When Kenneth opened the door he was almost driven back with the force of the wind, and almost suffocated with the soft, powdery, drifting snow. But he closed the door quickly after him and marched boldly on down the glen, rolling the end of his plaid about his neck, and at times having even to breathe through a single fold of it to prevent suffocation.

It was now well on in January. There had been but little snow all the winter, but this storm came on sharp and sudden. All day gigantic masses of cloud had been driving hurriedly over the sky on the wings of an easterly wind; the ground was as hard as adamant, and towards sunset the snow had begun to fall. But it took no time to settle on the bare ground; it was blown on and heaped wherever there was a bit of shelter from the fierce east wind. So it lay under the hedges and dykes, and on the lee-side of trees, and deep down in the ravines, and under banks and rocks, and across the road here and there in rifts like frozen waves of the ocean.

The wind howled terribly across the moorland. There was a moon, but it gave little light.

Kooran knew, however, where his master was going, and went feathering on in front, stopping now and then to turn round and give a little sharp encouraging bark to his sturdy young master.

Kenneth was all aglow when he reached Nancy's hut, and his face wet and hot. His hair and the fringes of the plaid and even his eyebrows were covered with ice.

He shook the plaid and his bonnet, and folded the former under the porch for Kooran to lie on. Then he opened the latch and entered.

All was dark. Not a blink of fire was on the hearth, and long white lines across the floor showed him where the snow had been sifting in through the holes that did duty as windows. Kenneth's heart suddenly felt as cold and heavy as lead.

"Nancy," he cried, "Nancy, oh! Nancy."

There was a feeble answer from the bed in the corner.

He advanced towards it. There were two shining lights there, the cat's eyes. Poor pussy was on the bed watching by her dying mistress.

He felt on the coverlet and found Nancy's hand there. It was cold, almost hard. "Nancy," he said, "it is Kennie, your own boy Kennie; don't be afraid."

It did not take long for Kenneth to light a roaring fire on the hearth. As soon as it burned up he held the iron lamp over it to melt the frozen oil; then he hung it up. The water in a bucket was frozen, and even some milk that stood on a little table near Nancy's bed was solid.

The inside of that cot was dreary in the extreme, but Kenneth soon made it more cheerful.

Poor old Nancy smiled her thanks and held out her hand to her boy, as she always called Kennie. He chafed it while he entreated her to tell him how she felt.

"Happy! happy! happy!" she replied, "but, poor boy, you are shaking."

Kenneth was, and he felt his heart so full that tears would have been a relief, but he wisely restrained himself.

He melted and warmed the milk, and made her drink some. Then, at her own request, he raised her up in the bed.

"Dinna be sorry," she said, "when poor auld Nancy's in the mools. It is the gate we have a' to gang. But oh! dear boy, it's the gate to glory for poor Nancy. And so it will be for you, laddie, if you never forget to pray. Prayer has been the mainstay and comfort o' my life; God has always been near me, and He's near me now, and will see me safe through the dark waters o' death. Here's a little Bible," she said. "It was Nancy's when young. Keep it for her sake, and oh! never forget to read it.

"Now, laddie, can you find your way to Dugald's? Send him here. There is an aulder head on his shoulders than on yours, and I have that to say a man should hear and remember."

"I'll go at once," said Kenneth, "and come back soon, and bring the doctor too, Nancy. I won't say good-night, I'll be back so soon."

Kenneth gulped down his tears, patted her hand, and rushed away.

"Come on, Kooran," he cried. "Oh! Kooran, let us run; my heart feels breaking."

He took his way across the moor in a different direction from that in which he had come. The storm had abated somewhat. The wind had gone down, and the moon shone out now and then from a rift in the clouds.

He determined to take the shortest cut to Dugald's house, though there would be the stream to ford, and it must be big and swollen. Never mind; he would try it.

He soon reached a scattered kind of wood of stunted trees; there was no pathway through it, but he guided himself by the moon and kept going downhill. He would thus strike the river, and keeping on by its banks, ford wherever he could.

Nothing could be easier. So he said to himself, and on he went. It was very cold; and though the wind was not so fierce, it moaned and sighed most mournfully through the trees in this wood. Even Kooran started sometimes, as a spruce or Scottish fir tree would suddenly free itself from its burden of snow as if it were a living thing, free itself with a rushing, crackling sort of sound, and stand forth among its fellows dark and spectre-like.

Kenneth had gone quite a long way, but still no stream came in sight. He listened for the sound of running water over and over again, and just as often he seemed to hear it, and went in that direction, but found it must be only wind after all.

He grew tired all at once, tired, weak, and faint, and sat down on a tree stump, and Kooran came and licked his cheek with his soft warm tongue. He placed one hand in the dog's mane, as if to steady himself, for his head began to swim.

"I must go on, though," he muttered to himself. "Poor old Nancy. The doctor. I'll soon be back—I—"

He said no more for a time. He had fainted. When he recovered, he started at once to his feet.

"I've been asleep," he cried. "How could I!" He ate some snow; then he began to move on automatically, as it were, the dog running in front and barking. The dog would have led him home. "No, no, Kooran," he said; "the river, doggie, the river."

Kenneth tried to run now. His teeth were chattering with the cold, but his face was hot and flushed.

His nerves had become strangely affected. He started fifty times at imaginary spectres. Some one was walking on in front of him—some shadowy being. He ran a little; it eluded him. Then he stopped; he was sure he saw a head peering at him over a piece of rock. He called aloud, "Archie! Archie!"

His voice sounds strange to his own ears. He runs towards the rock. There is no one behind it. No one. Nothing.

He feels fear creeping over his heart. He never felt fear before.

But still he wanders on, muttering to himself, "I'll soon be back. Poor old Nancy! Poor old Nancy!"

All at once—so it seems—he finds himself at the banks of a stream. He is bewildered now, completely. He presses his cold hand against that burning brow of his.

What is this river or stream? Where is he going? Did he cross this stream before? He must cross it now, but where is the ford? How deep and dark and sullen it looks.

He seats himself on the icy bank to think or try to think.

He is burning, yet he shivers.

Stories of water-kelpies keep crowding through his mind, and the words and weird music of a song he has heard,—

> "Kelpie dwells in a wondrous hall
>   Beneath the shimmering stream;
> His song is the song of the waterfall,
>   And his light its rainbow gleam.
>   The rowans stoop,
>   And the long ferns droop
>   Their feathery heads in the spray."

And now he jumps to his feet. He has recollected himself, he was going for the doctor for poor Nancy, and this is the stream he was looking for. He must seek the ford. He cannot have far to go now. Once over the river, and a run will take him to Dugald's cottage.

THE SCENE OF KENNETH'S NIGHT ADVENTURE.

But stay; what cares he for the ford? He will plunge into the deepest pool, and swim across. He is hot; he is burning; it will cool him.

He walks on a little way, and still the kelpie song runs in his brain. The trees seem singing it; the wind keeps singing it; the driving clouds nod to its music.

> "Where the foam flakes are falling,
> Falling, falling, falling,
> Falling for ever and ay—"

Ha! here is a deep dark pool at last. Why, yonder is the kelpie himself beckoning to him, and the maiden.

> "When forest depths were dim,
> For love of her long golden hair—"

The poor dog divines his intention. He rushes betwixt him and the cold black water, uttering a cry that is almost human in its plaintive pathos.

Too late. He laughs wildly, and plunges in. Then there is a strange sense of fulness in his head. Sparks crackle across his eyes.

> "Falling, falling, falling,
> Foam flakes are—"

He remembers no more.

But the brave dog has pulled him to the brink, and sits by his side, lifting his chin up towards the sky, and howling most pitifully.

Ah! if we only knew how much our faithful dogs love us, and how much they know in times of trouble and anguish, we would be kinder to them even than we are, even now, while sorrow smees far away from us.

Presently it appeared to strike even Kooran that giving vent to his grief would result in nothing very practical, so he suddenly ceased to whine. He bent down and licked his master's cold inanimate face.

He howled once again after this, as if his very heart were breaking.

Then he looked all round him.

No help, I suppose, he thought, could come from these cold woods, and no danger.

So he emitted one little impatient bark, as if his mind were quite made up as to what he should do, turned tail, and trotted off.

Chapter Eight
Kenneth and Jessie

"Will cannot hinder nor keenness foresee
What Destiny holds in the darkness for me."

Tupper.

Scene: Dugald's garden on the cliff top. You have to climb up to it from the road that goes winding through a wooded ravine, up a few steep gravel steps. It is spring-time, and the soft west wind goes sighing through the trees.

It is gloomy enough in the ravine below, but here the sun is brightly shining, and primroses are blooming on the borders, and the blue myosotis that rivals the noonday sky in the brightness of its colour.

On a wooden dais, near the keeper's door, Kenneth is lying rolled in his plaid and propped up with pillows. On the arm of the dais old Nancy's cat is seated, blinking in the sunshine and singing. On the pathway is Kooran, and book in hand—'tis Burns's poems—Archie is seated on a stone.

Kenneth's mother comes out and stands beside her boy, smiling and talking for a little, then goes in again. Dugald himself comes up the path, gun on shoulder, singing low, but he finishes the line in a louder voice when he sees Kenneth.

"'HOW BONNIE THE WOODS ARE.'"

"Ah, lad! out once more," he cries joyfully. "Och, man! it's myself that is glad to see you."

The moisture had gathered in the honest fellow's eye. Kenneth smiled faintly.

"You'll soon see me on foot again, the doctor says."

"But, man, if I live to be as auld as Methuselah, I'll never forget that dreary nicht your Kooran came howling to the door. He would hardly give me time to put my plaid on, and then he led me away and away to Brownie's Howe, and I found your body—there seemed no life in it—and carried you hame here on my shoulder.

"Ay, and Kooran has never left ye one hour since then, nor Nancy's cat either. She came here the very day after Nancy's funeral. Poor auld Nancy! How quietly she wore away. And how sensible she was to the last. And she told me a story about the laird, our dear laird McGregor, that you maunna hear noo, Kenneth. Good-bye. I'm off to the hills. Mind to keep the wind from him, Archie."

"How I should like to go too, Archie," said Kenneth.

"Oh!" said the boy, "that will soon be now. And oh! how bonnie the woods are, and the birds have all begun to build."

"Are the woods very bonnie, Archie?"

"Oh! delightful," cried the boy. "The moss is so soft and green under the trees. The wild flowers are creeping out and blowing on the banks. The pine trees are all stuck over with long white-green fingers."

"I know," said Kenneth.

"The birch tree stems are whiter than ever I saw them, just like silver, Kennie."

"Yes."

"And their branches are trailing down with the weight of their bonnie wee glittering leaves."

"Yes, yes."

"Then the needles on the larch trees were never so soft and green before, I'm sure, and they are just covered with red tassels."

"Yes."

"And the rowan trees (Rowan tree—the mountain ash) are covered with white flowers. What lots of scarlet roddans they'll have in autumn! And the birds are all building, as I said. I have a hoody-craw's nest in a Scotch fir in Alva, and a kestrel's in a terribly tall tree at Aultmore. That magpie is building a brand-new nest; I knew she'd have to."

"Well?"

"Well, there are five eggs in a laverock's among the corn, and I know where there is a ptarmigan's and a whaup's, far away up among the mountains."

"Oh! I do so long to be well, Archie."

"And the sheep, Archie?" continued poor Kenneth. "I've dreamed about them so often since I've been sick. I always see them lookin' up, Archie, with their bonnie brown een" (eyes), "and wonderin' what has come of me. And I'm sure Kooran wants to see them."

"Kooran could see them any day, and they're doin' finely, but Kooran won't leave you."

"Dear me, what shall I do?" cried Archie's mother, running distractedly up the garden with a bucketful of greens in her hand. To have seen her half-scared looks, one would have imagined something terrible was about to happen. "Gentry coming, and I'm no' dressed."

The gently arrived about five minutes afterwards, little Jessie, Miss Gale, and Miss Grant.

As soon as she found herself on the garden path Jessie, who had a bunch of primroses in her hand, and some long drooping crimson-tipped twigs from the larch, started to run. But she paused half-way, and an expression of sadness stole over her face, as she noticed how wan and white Kenneth was looking.

She advanced more slowly and tendered the flowers.

"Poor boy!" she said; "are you very, very ill?"

Kenneth took the flowers, and a flush of joy lit his pale cheeks as he replied,—

"Not now, Miss Jessie. The doctor says I have nothing to do but get well."

A SCENE IN INVERNESS-SHIRE.

"Oh, I'm so glad," cried Jessie.

Her governess now came up, and Miss Grant. The latter had been often before to see the invalid, but Jessie and Miss Gale had only recently arrived from Inverness-shire, and were loud in their praises of its magnificent scenery. Archie went and brought a chair for Jessie, so that she could sit while she talked to the invalid boy. Archie was improving. He even spoke to Jessie to-day, and promised to bring her something very nice if she would accept it. The something very nice ultimately proved to be a young hedgehog, so young that its spines had only just turned hard.

Presently the ladies went into the keeper's cottage. Archie lay down on the gravel-path with his head on Kooran's neck, and Jessie sat and talked to Kenneth.

What was she telling him? He looked intensely interested. His eyes were dilated, his hands clasped, his face flushed. It was but a simple story she was telling him, told in simple child's language. The story of her own London life, her life in society. But it was all, all so new to Kenneth.

Ah! little did innocent Jessie know that her prattle had lighted the fires of ambition in that boy's soul. But so it was. She had inaugurated a new phase in his existence. She had inadvertently led him to see that there were other—can I say better worlds than his?

So Jessie went away, with many a promise to come again when he was stronger, and could play soft melodies on the flute,—melodies, she said, that made her feel she wanted to cry, but that she loved all the same.

Jessie went away. She had found the boy on this bright lovely spring morning but a boy; she left him a man at heart.

Archie came and sat by him, and recommenced his tales of mountain and moorland and forest. He told him of the fairy knoll and the smugglers' cave, about the heather, now so green and promising, about early lambs, and all the little incidents of life in the hills. Kenneth listened, but his thoughts were far away.

These glens and wilds, dearly though he loved them, were not all the world. The poets and writers that had so charmed him hitherto, and served to throw a glamour of romance over the beautiful land in which he lived— Burns, Ossian, Tannahill, Campbell, Scott, and the Ettrick Shepherd,—they had made him love it, oh! so dearly love it, with that burning, passionate patriotism which only the heart can feel.

"That beats beneath a Scottish plaid."

But—had he not been living too much in the past? was there not a power setting in that was threatening to tear Scotland from the hands of the Scotch? Ought he to stay among these mountains and dream dreams, instead of going out into the world beyond to work or fight for the dear land that gave him birth? Ought he not to try even to gather wealth for the sake of those he would leave behind?

Clouds were gathering over the glen. A foreigner was soon to take possession of it, with no more love for the soil than if the heather that grew on every acre of it had not been dyed a hundred times over with the blood of the hero and the patriot. Could he stay at home and see his father's grave, poor old Nancy's too, levelled?

His thin hands covered his face, the boy sobbed quietly, and the tears trickled through his fingers.

Chapter Nine
The Storm Cloud Bursts over the Glen

"When simmer comes smilin' o'er mountain and lea,
The green haughs and glens are pleasant to see,
And pleasant the hum o' the merry wild bee,
When the rose, when the rose and lily are blawin'.
An' blithely the mavis salutes the gay morn
As sweetly he sings on the snawy white thorn,
While the laverock soars high o'er the lang yellow corn,
And the moorcocks, the moorcocks are cheerily crawin'."

Old Song.

Scene: Summer once more on hill and glen. On the mountain brow, the heather is bursting into bloom and bee-haunted. Down in the lower lands the corn is growing long and green, mingled with orange of marigold and crimson blush of wild poppy, and the meadows snowed over with gowan and scented clover. Fish leap gladly in stream and tarn, the lofty pines wave their dark plumes in the sunny air, and every wood and copse is filled with melody.

A right merry party are returning from the rocks by the seashore, where they have spent hours in wandering and wondering, for they found something new to admire at every turn.

Jessie is here with her governess and Miss Grant, and Kenneth strong and well again, to say nothing of Kooran and Shot, and last—probably least—Archie McCrane.

They have gained the brow of a hill overlooking the wide Atlantic. Far beneath them the sea-birds are wheeling and shrieking among the rocks, while out on the sea's blue breast is many a little white sail, some so far, far away that though they have three masts, and must therefore be mighty ships, they seem from here not a bit bigger than a sixpenny piece.

Little Jessie is looking radiant and lovely, Kenneth gallant and gay, and everybody else, always including the dogs, as healthy and happy as the summer's day is long.

Well, no wonder. They have spent such a gloriously pleasant day.

They took lunch with them to eat at sea. Yes, at sea, for old Duncan Reed took them out to the island and far beyond it, and Kenneth was proud on the whole to exhibit his skill as an oarsman. And Duncan had not hesitated to tell the ladies that he—Duncan Reed—had taught the boy all he knew about boating and fishing too.

The ladies were delighted with Duncan, especially Miss Gale, to whom he was something quite new. She must even sketch the little old man leaning there on his oar in his shirt-sleeves and night-cap, and Duncan was so delighted when he saw it, that his old eyes sparkled like the inside of an oyster-shell.

THE HILLS OVERLOOKING THE SEA.

He shared the luncheon, and when they landed they went to his strange house, with the boat for a roof, and there he made them tea, although there were not cups for all, and Duncan himself had to drink his out of a mug.

But there really was more in this little old fisherman than might at first appear. Anyhow he astonished Miss Gale by his recitations of Ossian's poems, both in the ancient Gaelic, and in English. Even Jessie, child though she was, experienced a thrill of indefinable pleasure as she listened to the rise and fall of the measured words, the magic of the wondrous verse, rolling out from the lips of this little old man, who looked so wild and weird, and mingling with the dull roar of the breaking waves.

The child never forgot it.

And now the little party stood on the hill overlooking the sea, and a walk of two miles took them, after a rest, to the fairy glen. But Archie, while they rested, had run on before, for everybody was coming to the cave, and Archie must see that it was neat and tidy.

There were freshly pulled ferns or brackens laid down as a carpet for the cave, and seats constructed out of the blooming heather. While making these Kenneth was thinking all the time about Jessie, and about how her eyes would sparkle when she saw these.

As they walked on over the hills, Kenneth by golden-haired Jessie's side, the sky above them blue and clear, the clouds on the horizon looking like snow-white feathers, and the bees making drowsy music among the pinky heath, Kenneth got his child-companion to talk and tell him more about the great world, that mighty ocean of life that lay in the far beyond, the ceaseless throb of whose billows was hardly ever heard among those peaceful hills.

The boy stopped and looked backwards and away out towards the sea. Probably he never looked half so handsome as he did now, with his heart filled with manly resolves, with the light of a half-kindled ambition making his face to shine.

"I'm very, very happy here, Miss Jessie," he said. "I may never, never be so happy as I am now, as I have been to-day. But before long I mean to leave this country, leave Scotland, and go away into the world, Miss Jessie."

The child looked at him half afraid.

"Yes, I'm foolish, I suppose, but I cannot help it; go I must. I daresay I have read too many books, but—I long to go."

"I'm going to take Nancy's Bible with me," he said, smiling and looking half ashamed. "I'll never part with that."

"Let me see it," said Jessie.

He took from his bosom a little old-fashioned Bible, with the Psalms of David—those heavenly gems of poetry and song—in metre at the end of the book, and placed it in the child's hand.

"You are a very good boy," she said, for the child felt she must say something.

"But oh!" she added, "here is a pressed primrose in the book."

"It is one of those you gathered for me; don't you remember?"

"Oh! yes," she replied, smiling, "but it looks so lonely; here, place this little tiny bit of heather beside it."

It was an innocent child-like action to place the bit of heather bloom there with the primrose, but one that Kenneth never forgot.

Archie was indeed a proud boy when Jessie and Miss Gale fell into raptures over the cave. Everything was admired, the heather seats, the rustic sofa, the rude bookcase containing the authors the boys read almost every day, and even the carpet of brackens.

"Did you get them?" said Kenneth in a stage whisper to Archie.

"Yes," replied Archie, with eyes as big as two-shilling pieces, "and such a fine lot they are. And the cream. Yes, and plates and spoons and all."

To the astonishment of his guests, Kenneth now placed a table in the centre of the cave, and bade them all sit down. Then from a dark recess he excavated a huge dish of mountain strawberries (Rubus chamaemorus), a jar of cream, and plates and spoons. Neither Jessie nor Miss Gale had ever eaten anything so delicious before.

"But what are they, Kenneth?" she said.

"They are called cloud-berries," replied Kenneth; "they only grow far up in the mountain tops, and some call them fairy food. People about here say that these berries creep in under their leaves, and hide when any one with a baneful eye looks at them, and that only good people can gather them."

"And who gathered these?" said Miss Gale.

"Archie."

"Oh! Archie, you are good."

Archie felt prouder even than before.

But after the cloud-berries were discussed, wee Jessie, sitting there on her heather couch, said, with a half-arch smile,—

"There is something else. Look at your tablets, Miss Gale."

"Oh yes," said Miss Gale. "Here it is—Flute."

Kenneth had the flute in his pocket. He was a marvellous player for a boy. His whole soul seemed to breathe through the instrument.

To-day he played a battle-piece of his own putting together—not composing.

First came the gathering of the clans, bold, energetic, soul-touching, then the plaintive farewell to native glens, as the Highlanders marched away,—

"Maybe to return to Lochaber no more."

Next came the spirited march, then the wilder pibroch as the foe was sighted, then wilder rushing music still; the fight was going on now, you could feel that. You could hear the shrill slogan of the Highlander mingling with shout of victor and shriek of wounded. Then a pause, and anon the coronach or wail for the dead.

And so the music died away.

Down the glen now the party went, for the sun was sinking low in the west, and the fairy glen was miles from the clachan.

But Jessie must see the sheep. Dugald was acting as shepherd to-day, and doffed his Highland bonnet as the ladies approached him.

There was not a sheep there that Kenneth did not know. They bleated a kindly welcome as he approached. They even played with Kooran, making great pretence to knock him down or to hit him with their hard feet, all of which Kooran took in good part, and kindly pretended to run from them, then turning and barking in a funny remonstrative voice, as if he really were laughing at heart, and enjoyed the fun immensely, and I have no doubt he did.

Dugald took Kenneth aside.

"There is bad news come," he said; "all is lost. The glen is to be evicted."

Kenneth's heart sank within him.

The cloud then that had been gathering so long was about to burst.

It was well-nigh a year since the tenantry had been asked to leave. They heeded not the summons. They could not believe that their own auld laird McGregor would send his people away. Little they knew. McGregor would never appear among them again. The edict sent through him was sent by or at the instigation of the new American laird. The glens were no good to him with people in them—so he said—he must have deer; he was buying the land for the "sport" it would afford him, his family and friends. Yet he doubted his own power, being a foreigner, to evict.

But that very day the last summons was given previous to forcible expulsion.

And the young men of the clachan and glens were wild. They would stand by their homesteads, they would grasp dirk and claymore, they would fight, they would die where they stood.

But at the great meeting that took place the wisdom of the grey-haired prevailed. And with sorrow, ay, and tears, they all came at last to the conclusion that resistance would be worse than useless.

They would not go till they were forced, they would stay and see the last of the dear old spot, but they would bend their necks to the yoke, they would maintain a passive attitude.

In this they showed their wisdom. The auld laird McGregor sent them a most affecting letter. "Their sorrows," it ended, "and his own misfortune had broken his heart, and though he could see them no more in life, his thoughts and mind were with them."

True, for the auld laird lived scarcely a year after the eviction of Glen Alva.

But with a portion of the remains of his fortune he paid the passage money to America of as many of his tenants as were willing to accept his offer.

I would not harrow the feelings of my readers by describing the last sad scene in Glen Alva, when in the darkness of night the people were turned out; when more than seventy houses—well, call them huts, they were homesteads, at all events—were given to the flames; when the aged and the sick were laid on the bare hillside to shiver and to die; and when neither the wail of the widow nor plaintive cry of the suffering infant could move to pity or mercy the minions of the Yankee laird, who preferred deer to human beings.

Selah!

Chapter Ten
The Last Link is Broken

"Farewell, farewell, my native land,
Thy lonely glens and heath-clad mountains."

Scene: The fairy glen once more, and in the background the fairy knoll. Kenneth and Archie, both looking very sad, are in the foreground by a new-made grave. Kenneth has been planting a little tree there, only a young Scotch pine, dug from the moor, a treelet that had grown from a cone which the rooks had fetched from Alva's gloomy forest. Kenneth has planted the tree, and the spade has dropped from his fingers and fallen among the heather.

Archie's dog Shot is standing near. He has been watching all the proceedings. Watching, and probably wondering. For dogs *do* think.

But where is Kooran? Kooran is under the sod. His bonnie brown eyes have closed for ever; his faithful heart will never feel love or friendship more—it has ceased to beat. Nor cry of wild bird on the mountain, nor plaintive bleat of lamb, no, nor his master's voice, will ever move him again.

"I canna but believe," says Hogg, the Ettrick Shepherd, "that dogs hae sowls."

There are many more believe with you, dear Hogg.

But about honest Kooran. When dogs get old, you know—and Kooran had got old before he died—a slight stiffness may be noticed in their gait. I am positive that they begin to wonder what ails them. Wonder why they cannot run so fast as they used to, in the good days of yore. Wonder why they get tired and out of breath so soon. Wonder, too, why master speaks so low, or why the sheep do not bleat so loudly or the birds sing so much as they used to. They do not know that this is only failure in their own powers of hearing. And they wonder also why the trees and grass and hedgerows have ceased to be so bright and green, even in spring-time, as once they were; why master's face seems dimmer. They cannot now stand the cold so well; they seem to want a thicker coat, but alas! the coat grows thinner. They would fain seek the shelter of indoors, even curl up on the hearthrug. How seldom do they get the chance! How often they receive the brutal kick when they most need comfort!

Then comes the day when they feel the cold no longer.

It had never occurred to Kenneth that some time or other Kooran and he must part—that Kooran must die. He was ever kind and attentive to this faithful friend of his; he never forgot him. He might have been excused if he had, for the scenes at the eviction and the burning of the glen were awful enough, in all conscience, to have driven everything else out of the boy's head.

Of all the houses in the glen, that alone of Kenneth's mother had been spared. Not that she meant to accept the favour thus offered her and stay on. Both she and Kenneth were far too proud for that. But at the cottage they lived for a time. And at the cottage Kooran died.

He came wet and weary one evening and threw himself down at his master's feet.

When Kenneth spoke to him he looked pleadingly up into his face and shivered. Kenneth had never seen him shiver before. The dog went and lay before the fire, and his master covered him up with his plaid. Kooran licked his hands.

Something, he knew not what, awoke the boy long before dawn next day, and his first thought was of his old favourite.

He peeped out at the little gable window in the garret where he lay. A pale scimitar moon was declining behind the trees. These looked black and spectre-like.

Kenneth went gently down the ladder, and lit the oil lamp. The fire was very low, and he replenished it. Then he gently lifted a corner of the plaid. The action aroused the dog, and he crawled forth. He seemed to feel for Kenneth's knee, and on this he laid his head.

Kenneth knew this was death. He put his hand tenderly on the poor dog's muzzle, for he could not hear him breathe.

The tongue came out to lick the hand. It was a farewell.

And the boys had rolled the body of poor Kooran in a piece of old tartan plaid, and, followed by Shot, carried him up to the fairy glen, and buried him near the fairy knoll. Remember they were only boys.

Then Kenneth sat down and cried. Archie had never before seen such an exhibition of weakness on the part of his friend, so what could he do but sit down and keep him company? They were only boys.

Shot looked very sad. He did not know what to make of it all. He whined impatiently. Then he licked Archie's wet face and touched Kenneth under the arm with his nose, as some dogs have a way of doing.

"Poor Shot!" said Kenneth. "You too have lost a faithful friend."

Together, after this, they took their way down the hill.

A short, crisp, and gentlemanly letter came to Kenneth two days after this. It was from Jessie's father.

"My daughter has spoken much about you," said this epistle, "and quite induced me to take an interest in your welfare. The situation of under-ghillie at my Highland shooting-box is vacant. I have much pleasure in placing it at your disposal. You will be good enough therefore to enter on your duties on Monday next, etc, etc."

Kenneth's cheek burned like a glowing peat. He tore the letter in fragments, and threw them in the fire.

"Mother," he cried, "dear mother, it needed but this! I shall leave the glen. I go to seek our fortune—your fortune, mother, and my own. I shall return in a few years as wealthy mayhap as the proud Saxon who now offers me the position of under-ghillie. Mother, it is best I should go."

I pass over the parting between the mother and her boy.

With his flute in his pocket, with no other wealth except a few shillings and his Bible, Kenneth McAlpine turned his back on the glen, and went away out into the wide, wide world to seek his fortune.

For years, if not for ever, he bade farewell to his Highland home and all he held so dear.

End of Book First.

Chapter Eleven
For Auld Lang Syne

"We twa have paddled in the burn
Frae mornin' sun till dine.
But seas between us broad hae rolled
Since the days o' auld lang syne."

Burns.

Scene: Landscape, seascape, and cloudscape.

    A more lovely view than that which met the eye of a stranger, who had seated himself on Cotago Cliff this evening, it was never surely the lot of mortal man to behold. It was on the northern shores of South America, and many miles to the eastward of Venezuela Gulf.

    Far down beneath him lay the white villas and flat-roofed houses of a town embosomed in foliage, which looked unnaturally green against their snowy walls. To the right, and more immediately below the spot where the stranger sat under the shade of trees, that towered far up into the sky, was a long, low, solitary-looking beach, with the waves breaking on it with a soft musical sighing sound; it was as if the great ocean were sinking to slumber, and this was the sound of his breathing.

SUNSET ON THE SEA.

The sun was low down in the west, in a purple haze, which his beams could hardly pierce, but all above was a glory which is indescribable, the larger clouds silver-edged, the smaller clouds encircled with radiant golden light, with higher up flakes and streaks of crimson. And all this beauty of colouring was reflected from the sea itself, and gave a tinge even to the wavelets that rippled on the silver sands.

It was very quiet and still up here where the stranger sat. The birds had already sought shelter for the night; well they knew that the sunset would be followed by speedy darkness. Sometimes there would be a rustle among the foliage, which the stranger heeded not. He knew it was but some gigantic and harmless lizard, looking for its prey.

"I must be going back to my hotel," he said to himself at last. He talked half aloud; there was no human ear to listen.

"I must be going home, but what a pity to leave so charming a place! I do not know which to admire the most, the grand towering tree-clad hills, the sea, or the forest around me.

"Hullo!" he added, "yonder round the point comes a little skiff. How quickly and well he rows! He must be a Britisher. No arms of lazy South American ever impelled a boat as he does his. Going to the hotel, I suppose. No, he seems coming straight to the beach beneath me. Hark! a song."

The rower had drawn in his oars, leaving the little boat to continue its course with the "way" already on her, while he gazed about him. Then, as if impelled to sing by the beauty around him, he trilled forth a verse of a grand old sea song.

> "The morn was fair, the sky was clear,
>   No breath came o'er the sea,
> When Mary left her Highland cot
>   And wandered forth with me.
> Though flowers bedecked the mountain side,
>   And fragrance filled the vale,
> By far the sweetest flower there
>   Was the Rose of Allendale."

Then there was silence once again. The rower rowed more slowly now, but soon he beached his boat, and drew it up, and hid it by drawing it in among the rocks.

The stranger soon afterwards rose to go.

He had not proceeded many yards along the hillside, when, on rounding a gigantic cactus bush, and close beside it, he stood face to face with the oarsman.

The former lifted his hat to bow, but instead of replacing it on his head he dashed it on the ground, and springing forward, seized the other by the hand.

"Archie! Archie McCrane!" he cried; "is it possible you do not know me, that you have forgotten Kenneth McAlpine?"

Poor Archie! for a moment or two he could not speak.

"Man!" he said at last, in deep, musical Doric; "is it possible it is you, Kennie?"

The tears were blinding him, both hearts were full, and they said no more for many seconds, merely standing there under the cactus tree holding each other's hands.

"God has heard my prayer," said Kenneth at last.

"And mine.

"But how you have altered, Kenneth! How you must have suffered to make you look so old!"

"You forget I *am* old, twenty-one next birthday; and you are only a year less. But what wind blew *you* here? I thought, Archie, you had settled down as an engineer on shore."

"Your letters roused a roving spirit in me, Kenneth. I determined to see the world. I took the first appointment I could get. On a Frenchman. I haven't had much luck. We have been wrecked at Domingo, and I came here last night in a boat. But come, tell us your own adventures. I have all your letters by heart, but I must hear more; I must hear everything from your own mouth, my dear brown old man."

Kenneth *was* brown; there was no mistake about that, very brown, and very tall and manly-looking, and the moustache he wore set off his beauty very much. No, he had not cultivated his moustache. It had cultivated itself.

"Come down to the hotel," said Archie. "I am not poor. We saved everything. It was a most unromantic shipwreck."

"No," replied Kenneth, "not to the hotel to-night. Come up the mountain with me to my cottage."

"Up the mountain?"

"Yes, my lad," said Kenneth, smiling. "Up the mountain. Haven't forgotten how to climb a hill, have you, I say, Archie, boy? for, as brown as I look, I am an invalid."

"What!" cried Archie, in some alarm. "Nothing serious, I sincerely hope."

"Nothing, old man, nothing. But when they left me here six weeks ago, I thought that no power could have saved me. I had yellow-Jack. That's all. I could not have lived in the hotel. Good as it is, it is too low. But come; old Señor Gasco waits supper for me."

Up and up they struggled, arm in arm. Kenneth knew every foot of the pathway through the forest; it was well he did, for night had quite fallen over sea and land, and the stars were glinting above them ere they reached a kind of tableland, and presently stood in front of the rose-covered verandah of a beautiful cottage.

The French windows were open, and they entered *sans cérémonie*. It was a lofty, large room, furnished with almost Oriental splendour, with brackets, ottomans, and suspended lamps, that shed a soft light over everything around.

And here were books, and even musical instruments *galore*, among the latter a flute. It was not the flute Kenneth used to play in Glen Alva, and up among the mountains, while herding his sheep; it was a far better one, but the sight of it brought back old times to Archie's memory.

Kenneth had left him for a few minutes.

Archie sank down upon an ottoman with the flute in his hand, and when Kenneth returned he found his friend in dreamland apparently.

But with a sigh Archie arose and followed Kenneth to an inner room.

"Señor Gasco," said the latter, "this is Archie McCrane, the friend of my boyhood, of whom you have so often heard me speak.

"Archie, this gentleman has saved my life. He is a kind of a hermit. Aren't you, *mon ami*?"

"No, no, no," cried Señor Gasco, laughing. "Only I love pure, fresh, cool air and quiet; I cannot get these in the town beneath, so I live here among my books."

He was a tall, gentlemanly-looking Spaniard, of some forty years or over, and spoke beautiful English, though with a slightly foreign intonation.

A supper was spread here that a king might have sat down and enjoyed.

Two tall black servants, dressed in snow-white linen, waited at the table. They were exceedingly polite, but they had rather larger mouths and considerably thicker lips than suited Archie's notions of beauty.

Out into the verandah again after supper, seated in rocking-chairs; the cool mountain air, so delicious and refreshing, was laden with the perfume wafted from a thousand flowers. There were the stars up in heaven's blue, and myriad stars, the fire-flies, that danced everywhere among the trees and bushes. Archie said they put him in mind of dead candles.

"And now for your story, Kenneth."

"It is a long one, but I must make it very brief. You know most of it, dear Archie, so why should I repeat it?"

"Because," said Archie, "I do *so* love to hear you speak. Your voice is not changed if your face is, and when I sit here in this semi-darkness, and listen to you, man, I think we are both bits of boys again, wandering through the bonnie blooming heather that clothes the hills above Glen Alva."

"Now you have done it," cried Kenneth, laughing.

"Done what?" said Archie.

"Why, *you* have to tell the first story. If you hadn't mentioned home, if you hadn't spoken about the hills and the heather, I would have told my tale first."

"But—" said Archie.

"Not a single excuse, my boy. I am home-sick now. Answer a few questions, and I'll let you off."

"Well, go on," said Archie; "ask away."

"My dear, dear mother! Have you seen her grave lately?"

"It was the last spot I visited when I went to the clachan," replied Archie sadly.

"Heigho!" sighed Kenneth. "And I was all ready to go home. We were lying at the Cape, if you remember, when your letter arrived. Yes, and I left my ship, I threw up a good appointment on receipt of the sad intelligence; and Archie, dear lad, I shall go back to Scotland when I make my fortune—not before, and that may be never."

"Do not speak like that."

"But I must and will. How changed everything must be from the time I kept the sheep among the hills. And how do the clachan, the glen, and the hills look now?"

"The clachan is but little changed. Mr Steve did not tear down the village and church, as he first threatened. No, the clachan is the same, but poor Mr Grant has gone."

"Dead! You did not tell me this in your letter."

"No, no, not dead. He has got a better living in the city."

"Yes?"

"Yes, and I went to see them. The Misses Grant keep every letter ever you wrote them, and they do long, I can tell you, for the return of the wanderer."

"Bless their dear hearts!"

"I went over to the wee village by the sea and saw Duncan Reed."

"Is he changed?"

"Not in the very least. Looks hardier than ever."

"And your father and mother you have already said are well?"

"Yes, but father doesn't like town life. How he would love the old days to come back again; how he would love to rove once again over the hills gun on shoulder and dog at his heel!"

"He is not very old; he may yet have his wish."

"I fear not."

"Well?"

"Well, the glens and hills all around are planted with trees. This was done as soon as Mr Steve took possession of the estate, and before poor old Chief McGregor died."

"He is dead, then?"

"Yes. I would have told you, but I wanted to make my letters to you as bright as possible."

"So the dear old man is dead. Heigho! And the estate planted. You did not even tell me that."

"No, and for the same reason. But the trees are getting quite tall already. Most of the higher parts of the glens are covered with Scotch firs and spruces and larches, the lower lands with elm and plane and scrubby oaks. At the risk of being taken as a trespasser, I went all over the estate. I penetrated up to the fairy knoll and saw poor Kooran's grave. There are young trees all round there now."

"Archie," said Kenneth, leaning forward and peering into his companion's face, "I hope they didn't interfere with poor Kooran's grave."

"No, nor with anything around it."

"Go on, lad; I'm so pleased."

"Well, I've little more to say. I was not taken prisoner, though I startled the wild deer in all directions."

"But the grand old hills themselves?"

"Nay, they are not planted. Green in summer and purple and crimson in autumn, there they are the same, and ever will remain."

There was a pause. Then Kenneth spoke once again.

"Did you ever see Miss Gale since?"

"Only once," replied Archie, "and Miss Redmond—Jessie—she has grown tall, and oh! Kenneth, so beautiful, but still so child-like and graceful."

"I can easily believe that, boy. And did she—"

"Yes, dear lad," said Archie. "She did ask all about you, so kindly. And I gave her your last letter to read. And—"

"And she read it, Archie? Tell me, did she read it?"

"Yes, she read it over and over again."

"Now, I'll tell you my own adventures."

"Begin at the beginning, won't you? The very beginning, from the day you and I parted."

"I will."

But what Kenneth said deserves a chapter to its own account.

Chapter Twelve
Kenneth and Archie

"Adieu, adieu; my native land
Fades o'er the waters blue;
The night-winds sigh, the breakers roar,
And shrieks the wild sea-mew.
Yon sun that sets upon the sea
We follow in his flight;
Farewell awhile to him and thee,
My native land, good-night."

Byron.

Scene: Kenneth and Archie still seated in the verandah of the Spaniard's cottage. The light from the casement window is streaming outwards through the creepers and climbing plants all around them; the beautiful bell-like flowers, down-drooping, touch their very faces. But all the colour up there in the verandah's roof does not belong to these flowers. No, for birds are sheltering their bright wings from the night dews; that rich orange spot in the corner is a bird, so is that patch of crimson and steel, and yonder one of snow-white and blue. If you looked steadily for a moment at them, you could see round heads turned downwards and wondering beads of eyes. The birds are considering whether or not all is safe, or whether they had better fly away out into the night and the darkness.

Kenneth is waiting for the Señor to come. There is hardly a sound except a gentle sighing of wind among the trees, now and then the shriek of a night bird, the constant chirp of cicada, or rap, rap, rap, of green lizard as he beats to death some unhappy moth he has captured.

"Now, Señor, come and sit you down. Light your great pipe. That is right. Thanks, yes, both Archie and I will have a little palm-leaf cigarette. Coffee? Oh! delightful! Archie: old man, there isn't any one in all the wide world ever made coffee half so well as the Señor Gasco. Flattery, Señor? No, not a bit of it. The truth cannot be flattery."

"The coffee," said Archie, "is delicious."

"Heigho!" sighed Kenneth. "I am so happy to-night, dear Archie. I believe it will really do me good to tell you of some of the troubles I have come through; it will dilute my joy.

"I don't know, Archie, old man, how ever I became a sailor. I'm not quite sure, mind you, that I am altogether a sailor yet at heart, though I dearly love the sea, and a roving life is *the* life for a man of my temperament. Señor is smiling; he will never admit I am a man. But I have come through *so* much, and the years I have spent since I left the dear old glen have been indeed eventful, and seem a long, long time.

"But, Archie, lad, when I began my wanderings through the world, I can tell you my ambition was very great indeed. I determined, you know, to make my fortune, and I determined to make it in a very short time. The details of the process of fortune-manufacture, however, didn't present themselves to me, all at once anyhow. I turned my back on Glen Alva, and so full was my heart that I put at least ten miles behind me before I sat down to rest. I got inside a wood at last, and seated myself beneath a tree, and counted my money, three shillings and fivepence-halfpenny! Well, many a man has begun the world on less.

"But this money couldn't last long. What then should I do? I'll tell you what I did do. I fell sound asleep, and the sun was setting when I awoke, and flooding all the wood with mellow light.

"There was a blackbird came and perched half-way up a neighbouring spruce tree and began fluting.

"'Oh!' I said half aloud, 'two of us can flute.'

"So the blackbird and I piped away there till it got nearly dark. But I felt hungry now, and music is not very filling, Archie. So I put up my flute and started to my feet; I felt stiff now, but it soon wore off.

"I went on and on and on, getting hungrier every minute, but there was no sign of village or house. I drank some water from a rill that came tumbling down through a bank of ferns, and felt better.

"I was beginning to wonder where I should sleep, when the sound of merry laughing voices fell upon my ear. The party, whoever it was, came rapidly on towards me from among the trees.

"'Hullo, lad!' said one; 'are ye comin' to the dance?'

"'Dance!' I cried; 'why, my feet are all one bag of blisters, and I'm faint with hunger. Dance, indeed!'

"'It's a puir beggar laddie,' said a girl, whose face I could hardly see in the uncertain light.

"'Beggar!' I exclaimed. 'Who d'ye call a beggar? I've a whole pocketful of money, only I've lost the road.'

"'Come along, then,' they all cried. 'Come along with us.'

"And off we all went singing. We struck off the road down across the fields, and soon I heard the music of a fiddle and saw bright lights. A young man came out of a farmhouse to welcome us. He told us dolefully that only one fiddler had come, and plaintively asked what could be done.

"'I've a flute,' I cried.

"'Hurrah!' they answered. 'Come in, my boy.'

"'The laddie maun eat first,' said the girl who had called me a beggar.

"I blessed her with all my heart, though not in words.

"What a supper they gave me! And didn't I eat just! I could play now, and we spent such a joyful night, and dawn was breaking and the blackbirds up and fluting again long before the merry party broke up.

"I got a bed and slept far into the day; then, after a good dinner from these kind-hearted farm folks, I began my journey in search of fortune once more.

"By evening I saw great grey clouds lying in the hollows before me. It was smoke. I was nearing Glasgow, and in two hours more I was walking along the Broomielaw.

"I had never seen so many people before in my life, but hardly anybody looked at the shepherd lad in Highland garb. I determined they should, though. I put my flute together, and standing near the bridge, commenced to play 'The Flowers of the Forest.'

"Was it the singular plaintiveness of this beautiful air, I wonder, or was it that my thoughts were away back again in the glen I had left, and with those I loved so dearly? I do not know, but I seemed to become oblivious to everything. My very soul was breathed into the music; I was speaking and appealing to the crowd through the instrument.

"The crowd! Yes, there was a crowd. I became aware of that as soon as I had finished, and money, piece after piece, was forced into my hand. I took the money. I felt ashamed of it next moment, but to have gone off then would have seemed ungrateful. I played still another air. Again I paused.

"'No more money,' I cried aloud as I fled away.

"They must have thought the Highland boy was mad.

"Some time afterwards I found myself standing at a book-seller's window looking at a picture, a ship, a gallant ship in a gale of wind.

"A GALLANT SHIP IN A GALE OF WIND."

"How I longed to be at sea then! How I hated the bustle and stir and talking and noise all round me! That splendid ship—the sea was wild and rough all around her, the spray dashing over her bows; there would be the roar of the wind through rigging and shroud, and the wild scream of sea bird rising high over the dash of the waves. She bore it well; the sheets were taut; the sails were rounded out and full. How I longed to be at sea!

"A hand was laid on my shoulder. I started and looked up. No need to start.

"A kindly face looked down into mine.

"'You are in grief of some kind, my boy,' he said, this white-haired old gentleman. 'Nay, don't be too proud to admit it. Pride has been the downfall of the Highland race.'

"'If you please, sir,' I replied, boldly enough now, 'the Highlanders are not a downfallen race.'

"'I did not mean it in that way,' he said, smiling at my vehemence. 'But come with me, boy; I know we will be friendly.'

"Where he took me, or what he said to me, I need not tell you.

"Suffice it to say that next day we left Scotland and journeyed south by rail, and I wept—yes, I do not now think it shame to say so, though I struggled then to hide my tears—I wept to cross the border.

"'It will be such a pleasant change for you, my dear boy,' said good old Major Walton—for that was the gentleman's name, and he had quite taken to me after hearing all my story—'a delightful change indeed after your own bleak, cold, wild hills. We have a very pretty home in Hampshire. You'll soon forget you were ever anywhere else.'

KENNETH'S ENGLISH HOME.

"The Major's home was indeed a very nice one; close to the borders of the New Forest it was, and not a great way from the sea.

"But ah! Archie, lad, everything was very foreign to me; the very trees looked strange and uncouth, especially the docked pollards, that stood by the banks of the sluggish streams. The style of the houses was strange to me, and the lingo and talk of the people, who, in my opinion, were terribly ignorant.

"The Major was kindness itself, and so were his wife, her sister, and two children. The major had but one hobby—music. He played the violin himself, and he told me honestly that his chief reason for 'taking me'—these are his very words—was because I played with such feeling.

"My evenings were happy enough in this English home of mine; my days I spent in the garden, where I was allowed to work, or in the great forest. You must not imagine, Archie, the New Forest is anything like a deer forest in our own land. There are in it no wild mountains, no deep dark dells, no beetling crags and cliffs, no cataracts, no foaming torrents; the red deer does not toss his wide antlers here and fly proudly away at your approach, nor far above you in the sky do you see the bird of Jove circling upwards round the sun.

"Wilson would never have said about the New Forest,—

"'What lovely magnificence stretches around!
Each sight how sublime, how awful each sound;
All hushed and serene, like a region of dreams,
The mountains repose 'mid the roar of the streams.'

"But many a long day I spent roaming about in this forest, nevertheless.

"I was charmed with the solitary grandeur of the place. I had no idea it was so extensive either, or so varied in its beauties. Why, here one might wander about for weeks and never weary, for he would always be coming to something new. Is this the reason, I wonder, that it is called the *New Forest*? New in point of time it certainly cannot be termed, for everything in it and about it is old, extremely old. The oaks are gnarled and wrinkled, and grey with age; its elms and its ash trees, its limes and its alders, are bent and distorted by the touch of time, and the lichens that cling to their stems only add to their general appearance a look of hoariness that is far from unpleasing to the eye.

"Then the heather which covers the large sweeps of moorland that you see here and there is very sturdy and strong, while from the furze or whins boats' masts could be made.

"The creatures, too, that one sees while walking through this forest, seem birds and beasts of some bygone time, and look as if they hardly, if ever, saw a human being from one year's end to the other.

"The hares or rabbits, instead of scurrying away at your approach, sit leisurely on one end while they wash their faces and study you. The blackbirds and the mavises hardly trouble themselves to cease their song even when you walk close by the trees on which they are perched. The great beetles and other members of the coleoptera tribe are far too busy to take the slightest notice of your presence, and the great velvety bees go on working and humming just as if there were no such creature as you within a thousand miles of them.

"Then the voles or water rats that live in the depths of this truly English forest are not the least curious specimens of animal life to be found therein. If you happen to be reclining anywhere near a pool that by long-established custom belongs to them alone, before many minutes one, if not two of them, will come out to stare and wonder at you; they, like the hares, sit up on one end to conduct their scrutiny; and they gaze and gaze and gaze again, digging their finger joints or knuckles into their eyes, in a half-human kind of a way, to squeeze out the water, and clear their sight for one more wondering look."

(My country readers, who love nature, must have noticed the voles at this queer performance.)

"What is he at all? Where did he come from? What is he going to do? These are the questions those voles seem trying in vain to solve.

"Here in this New Forest is a silence seldom broken save by the song of bird or cry of some wild creature in pain, while all around you is a wealth of floral beauty and verdure that is charming in the extreme.

"Yes, Archie, I came ere autumn was over to love that forest well. I was not selfish enough, though, to keep all the pleasures of it quite to myself, and the Major's children often accompanied me in my rambles. I used to read Burns and Ossian to them. They liked that, but they liked the flute far better. It appealed straight to their senses.

"But when autumn passed away, when the leaves fell, and the fields were bleak and bare, at night, when the wind moaned around the house which I now called home, then, Archie, I used to dream I heard the surf beating in on the rugged shores of my native land. I would start and listen, and long to be once more in Scotland.

"THE RUGGED SHORES OF MY NATIVE LAND."

"I went, one day, to the forest all alone; I went to think.

"'What are you staying here for?' perhaps said one little thought. 'Major Walton may leave you money when he dies.'

"I smothered that thought at its birth, and crushed many more like it.

"Kind good old Major Walton! I must tear myself away; I must be independent; I must push my own way in the world.

"'Heaven help me to do so,' I prayed. Then I took out the little old Bible Nancy had given me, Archie, and I found some comfort there.

"I was putting it back again in my bosom when a little card dropped out; I picked it up. On it were pressed these, Archie."

Kenneth took the Book from his breast as he spoke, and opening it, handed the card to Archie.

"I know," said the latter: "the primrose and the bit of heather."

"Yes, dear boy, foolish of me, I know; but I have never parted with them, and if I go to Davy Jones's locker—as we sailors say—if I am drowned, Archie, these flowers will sink with me.

"But on that winter's day in the forest, Archie, these flowers seemed to speak to me, or rather the golden-haired child spoke to me through these flowers. I was back again on the hills above Glen Alva walking by her side; the sky above us was blue and clear, the clouds on the horizon looking like snow-white feathers, and the bees making drowsy music among the pinky heath.

"I started up, and the vision fled, and around me were only the bare bleak forest trees and the fading heather. The vision fled, but it left in my breast the desire stronger now than ever to make my own way in the world, by the blessing of Providence; and Providence has never deserted me yet, Archie, lad.

"I went straight home. I saw Major Walton, and talked to him, and told him all.

"He seemed sorry. The last words he said to me when I went away—and there was moisture in the old man's eyes as he spoke—were these:—

"'Mind, I'm not tired of you, and I hope to live to meet you once again.'

"I went to Southampton next day. I thought I had nothing to do but march on board some outward-bound ship, that they would be glad to have me.

"Alas! I was disappointed."

(The author hopes some boy who meditates running away to sea may read these lines.)

"I was rudely jostled and laughed at, I was called a Scot, a Sawnie, a Johnny-raw, but work was never once offered me.

"I wandered about the streets, not knowing what to do. The few coins I had in my possession did not last many days.

"I felt sad and unhappy. I felt almost sorry I had left the good people who had done so much for me. The 'bairnies' had been in tears when I went away; even the black-and-tan terrier had followed me a long way down the road, and looked very 'wae and wistfu'' at me with his brown beseeching eyes when I said he must go back.

"For two whole days I had hardly anything to eat. My flute, that I was fain to fall back upon, failed to support me, for the English, Archie, have not so much music and romance in their souls as the Scotch have. But one thing the English have is this, Archie, sound common-sense and a love of derring-do.

"I was standing one day on the pier at Plymouth. I had played my way with my flute all this distance in the hopes of getting a ship. I was no more successful than before.

"On this particular day, Archie, the drum was up (the storm signal), the wind blew cold and high, and the seas tossed their white manes as they rushed each other up the bay. I was feeling very sad and disconsolate, when all at once I heard a voice say to a man beside me,—

"'I'll give a guinea to be taken out to yonder ship.'

"'I don't care to win no guinea,' said the fellow addressed, a hulking boatman in a rough blue jersey. 'I don't care to win no guinea on a day like this. 'Sides, sir, I hain't got no mate.'

"'I'll go,' I cried.

"'You!' said the gentleman; 'why, you're but a child.'

"'I'm a Scotch boy,' I replied, 'and I know boating well.'

"'All right, my lad; jump in.'

"It took us nearly an hour, but we did it.

"I was very wet, and the gentleman kindly took me below, and gave me warm coffee.

"'Now,' he said, 'I'm going to give you half a guinea, and the man half, for if he has to change the gold, he will cheat you.'

"'Are you captain of this ship, sir?' I asked.

"'I am, lad; I'm all that is for the captain.'

"'Well, sir,' I said, 'give the man all the guinea, and take me with you as a boy.'

"I then told him all my story.

"'We don't sail for a week,' he said, 'and if in that time you get your mother's consent, I'll be glad to have so plucky a youngster on board my craft.'

"My dear mother gave her consent, as you know, Archie; and so I became a sailor and a wanderer."

I have but epitomised Kenneth's story. He took much longer time to tell it than I, the author of this little book, am doing, and besides, there was much conversation interspersed with it betwixt him and his old friend Archie.

The moon was high up above the forest trees before he finished, shedding a flood of golden light over mountain and sea, so, promising to resume his narrative next evening, Kenneth arose, and soon after all was silent and dark inside this peaceful cottage.

Chapter Thirteen
Kenneth's Story (continued)—At the Cave

"On, on the vessel flies; the land is gone,
And winds are rude in Biscay's sleepless bay;
Four days are sped, but with the fifth anon,
New shores descried make every bosom gay."

Byron.

Scene: The Spanish Señor and his two guests, Kenneth and Archie, once more together, not in the mountain cottage to-night, but in a cave, close down by the edge of the sea. It was the sea that was lisping on the sands not far from where they sat on the rocks, but the view beyond was one of moonlight, trees, rocks, and water combined, altogether very beautiful, and in some respects almost English-like.

Yes, now by moonlight it looked thoroughly English, but if by day you had rowed round these rocks, you would soon have been undeceived, for sharks in dozens visited the deep water, and in the cracks beyond were alligators, active and strong, and very hideous-looking crabs often crawled up the wet black cliffs; and among the trees themselves were great snakes, deadly and venomous; but it all looked very quiet and lovely now.

A MOONLIGHT SCENE.

Kenneth was fond of caves, and there were plenty of them about here. He kept his boat in one. That very day, together the two friends had launched it, and spent all the long hours of sunlight in sailing or rowing about among the lovely islands of this sparkling sea, that look on a calm day as if they were actually afloat not in the water, but in the sky itself.

"My life," said Kenneth, resuming his narrative of the day before, "my life, I thought, was going to be all rose-tinted now.

"Alas! Archie, lad, I soon found it quite the reverse, and it does really seem to me that those writers of books who paint a sailor's existence as one long picnic do grievous wrong to the young folks who read them.

"A sailor's life is like the billowy ocean on which he resides, all ups and downs, Archie."

"I can easily believe that," said his friend.

"But Captain Pendrey was very good to me, and there was an old boatswain on board who became my friend from the very first. He taught me to reef, to splice, and to steer, ay, and a deal more; in fact, during the two years I sailed in the old *Miranda*, he made a man of me.

"You see, Archie, I was already so far a seaman that I was not afraid of the ocean; and I was good at an oar.

"I was downright seasick when I first went out of Plymouth Sound. We had a head wind, and being only a sailing craft, had to beat and beat for days. I didn't care much then what became of me. But the rough old bo'sun came and shook me up—I was lying nearly dead on a sea-chest—'Pull yourself together, youngster. Go on deck,' he said, 'and look at the waves. Ain't they mountains, just! It won't do to give in.'

"I did go on deck and look at the waves, just for a moment. A green sea came thundering over the bows, took me off my legs, and washed me away down into the lee-scuppers, where I would have been drowned if the bo'sun hadn't caught me up.

"'I'm not going below again, though,' I said to myself.

"Nor did I.

"The boats were all on board; I got into one of these as night fell, lashed myself to a thwart, and wet though I was, I slept with my head on a coil of ropes all through that stormy night. Stiff in the morning? Yes, a little, but I was better. I got my clothes off, and a man dashed buckets of sea water over me, and this revived me so much that I went below.

"The men in my mess were at breakfast; they were sitting on deck, jammed into corners anyhow, with their sou'wester hats between their legs to steady their coffee mugs.

"'Salt pork, my lad,' said the bo'sun. 'You're just at that stage that salt pork will turn the scale.'

"I took the hunk of pork he gave me and devoured it.

"Well, the bo'sun was right. It did turn the scale with a vengeance: I went on deck and hove the lead apparently. The steward passed me and said,—

"'You're not sick, are you, Sandie?'

"'No,' I said, 'I'm only shamming. Ugh!'

"But by the time we were over the bay I was as sea-fast as any one on board. I got my sea legs, too.

"How blue the sea was now! How white the birds that skimmed over its surface! And the sails of ships that appeared in the distance were like snow when the sun shone over them.

"It wasn't all sunshine even then, for a smart breeze was blowing, and cloud shadows chasing each other over the sea, just as I had often seen them do over fields of ripening grain in Glen Alva.

"I settled down to sea-life very easily now and very naturally. I soon knew every rope and spar and bolt in her, and was as happy as the sea-gulls. I cannot say more.

"We touched at Madeira, and here the captain took me on shore, and all over the place. What an isle of romance and beauty it is!

"We called in both at Saint Helena and Ascension, the former not the lonely sea-girt rock that old books describe, but a charming island of mountain, strath, and glen. Nor did I find Ascension to be a cinder with a few turtles on its beach. It has been cultivated to a wonderful extent, and I never did see a bluer, brighter ocean than that which laves its shores. The Cape of Good Hope hove in sight at last. I watched its bold and rugged coast as we came nearer and still more near to it.

"It was but like a long irregular cloud lying along the horizon at first. Then this cloud grew higher and darker and more defined. Then it grew bluer in parts, and lines stood boldly out towards us, then it turned blue and purple, oh! so lovely, and last of all it was a cloud no longer, but mountains stern and wild, and braelands covered half-way up with purple heath and wild flowers—geraniums I found afterwards these were—with rocks on the shore and a long white line of surf and sand.

"We did our business at the Cape and bore up for Australia.

"What a stretch of sea we had to cross, and what a length of time it was ere we reached Sydney!

"But I was not idle all these months. It was so good of Captain Pendrey, but he seemed to take a delight in teaching me navigation. He flattered me, too, I fear.

"'You're far too good and bright a boy,' he said, 'to stick before the mast.'

"So I worked and worked not only to please him, but because there was a prospect of my one day walking on the snowy quarter-deck of some beautiful barque, her proud commander.

"Every one on board loved our captain, although they called him the old man behind his back. From Australia we went to Hong Kong, then to Ceylon, from there to Calcutta, and then back again to Ceylon, and returned to India, lying up for repairs at the city of Bombay. And my kind captain never once went on shore without taking me with him, so that I saw so much that was strange in life, lad, that I could sit and talk in this cave for a month if my good friend here would bring us prog, and then I wouldn't have half told you all my strange experiences.

THE BURNING SHIP.

"I had been now nearly two years at sea, and had passed one examination, so things were looking up.

"I dearly loved the sea and sea-life now. I would not have changed places with a land-lubber for all the world.

"We had many narrow escapes, of course, for our ship was a clipper, and the captain 'cracked on.' He did not mind risk so long as he made good voyages. But somehow I never dreamt of danger, not even while in the centre of a tornado in the Indian Ocean at night, and if there be a more fearful experience than that in the life of a mariner, I have yet to encounter it.

"Nor did I dream of danger even when seated of a night under the bright stars at the fo'c'stle head, while the men spun yarn after yarn of the awful dangers they had come through.

"'I've been wrecked often and often,' said our old 'bo'sun' one night. 'I was in the *Bombay* when she was burned; I was a man-o'-war's man then. Ah! Kennie, lad, it is a fearful thing, a fire at sea. I hope you'll never see a burning ship. Over seventy of my shipmates were doomed that night, and some of them met worse deaths than drowning.

"'Another time,' he went on, 'I was the only one saved out of a gunboat. I was taken off a bit of wreckage and rigging by the lifeboat after drifting about for twelve wet, cold, weary hours. Strange thing was this. I had been made captain of the foretop only a week before we were wrecked. 'Tis funny, mate, but it was on that same foretop I floated about so long. He! he! I was captain of the foretop then, and no mistake, and monarch of all I surveyed.'

"Just three weeks after this particular evening, Archie, I was away aloft one beautiful day. We were well down over the line, and bearing about South-South-East.

"There was a kind of haze over the ocean that day which made seeing distinctly difficult at any great distance, but I noticed what at first sight I thought was a bird or a shark's fin. I hailed the deck as soon as I made out it was something afloat with men on it.

"'Where away?' came the reply.

"On pointing in the direction, the yards were trimmed, and we soon got nearer.

"The sight that met my eyes I will not forget till my dying day. The survivors of a ship that had foundered they were, half-naked, half-dead, sun-blistered, sinking wretches, five in all.

"They had been afloat on a raft for nine days without food to eat, and with hardly a drop of water to quench their awful thirst.

"From that day, Archie, I began to think that a sailor's life had its dark as well as its rosy side.

"A year after this grief came. We were homeward bound. We got nearly to the Cape, and there our ship was dashed on a lee-shore, and I lost two of the best friends ever I had at sea, our poor captain and the dear old bo'sun.

"I was landed at Symon's Town at last, and there, Archie, I got your letter, and found I was an orphan. And all this great grief came to me within a fortnight.

"I had been bound for English shores; my hopes beat high; in a few months longer, at most, I would once again clasp my dear mother in my arms, once more visit my home. Changed I knew the glen would be, but old friends would give me a warm greeting.

"Heigho! the blow fell; I determined not to return, and, Archie, from that day to this I have been a wanderer.

"But bless Providence for all His mercies! Archie, lad, I'm not badly off, and I have you.

"Shake hands, old boy. Now I've been doing all the talking, I shall take it out of you next, for I dearly love to hear your voice.

"Señor Gasco, *mon ami*, suppose we launch our little boat, and be off. I'm longing for supper and longing to sit down and rest in our mountain cottage. I don't think I've been so happy for many and many a long year.

"Come along, Archie. How lovely the moonlight is playing over the water!"

Chapter Fourteen
Friday Night at Sea

"Now round the galley fire the merry crew,
With song and yarn and best of cheer,
Have gathered. And storms may rage, and seas may rise,
And thunders roll; they know not fear."

Anon.

Scene: A ship at sea, south of the Cape of Good Hope. A steamer evidently from her build, though the funnel has been lowered, and a gale of wind is roaring through her rigging, bellying out the few sails she is able to carry till it looks as though the cloth would bust. She is making heavy weather, dipping the ends of her long yards right into the water, and plunging so much, that at times neither her jib-boom nor bows are visible in the foam and spray. She must be shipping tons of water. Looking at her as we are now doing with the eye of imagination, it would seem there could be little else save discomfort on board of her. And the night, too, is closing around her dark and thick. The sea is very troubled, the waves are racing, brawling, foam-crested billows, lightning plays around the ship every now and then, and thunders hurtle in the air, the awful noise appearing to run along over the sea. But let us go on board of her.

Here are Kenneth and Archie. Neither is on duty. Kenneth's watch will come on deck at midnight. Archie, who is engineer of this craft, may be called upon at any moment to stir up the banked fires and get up steam.

This is the ship in which Kenneth has been second mate for eighteen months, including the time he lay sick or roamed convalescent on the South American shore, where Archie found him. They have bidden farewell to that beautiful coast, which in some parts is so enchanting, with its wealth of vegetation, its grand old woods, its fruit trees, its flower-trees, its flowers themselves, the life and loveliness that teems everywhere on the earth, in the air, in the sea, on the little islands, green and feathery, that peep up here and there out of the blue, on mountain top, and even in its caves, that I feel sad as well as sorrowful. I cannot pause to describe it all.

But why should I? My descriptions, after all, would fall flat on the senses of the reader, even with the aid of the best of illustrations, for no artist can give colour and movement combined. Go, reader, and see the world for yourself if you feel so inclined, and if ever you have the chance, I can tell you from long experience it is a very beautiful one.

"Well," said Kenneth, "we came up here, Archie, lad, to have a walk, but I don't see much chance. What a night it is going to be! How black the sky! How vivid the lightning! How close the horizon is—"

The last part of Kenneth's sentence was lost in a peal of thunder.

"Stand by! Jump, Archie. There is a comber."

They both leapt on the top of the capstan as an immense green sea swept over the bows and came tearing aft, carrying everything movable before it.

When it passed away, and the water found partial exit by the scuppers,—

"I don't think there will be much pleasure in a walk to-night, Kennie," said Archie. "Wouldn't I like to be back again on that flower mountain of yours!"

"Poor dear old Gasco!" said Kennie with a sigh. "You find good among people of all nations."

"He was very sad when you bade him good-bye."

"Yes, and I won't forget his last words. They are so true 'Farewell,' he sighed rather than said, 'farewell, if farewell it must be. This meeting to part, and meeting *but* to part with those one gets to love, is one of the most soul-sobering feelings attached to our lot here below. Ah!' he continued, lifting up a finger—you know his style, Archie—'Ah! my young friend, what a joyful place heaven must be, if only for this one reason, we shall meet all our dear, dear friends again, and parting will be unknown! Farewell; we'll meet Yonder, if not on earth again.'"

There was a pause in the conversation, filled in by the whistling wind and the ceaseless rush of the dashing waves.

"Well," said Archie at last, "I cannot say that a night like this, Kennie, makes one feel enamoured of a sailor's life."

"You must take the shadow as well as the sunshine, though," returned Kenneth. "You would rather be back at my boathouse cave, I daresay, at Cotago, launching the tub for a pleasant day among the islands, wouldn't you?"

"Yes, indeed. Stand by; there is another wave."

"Hark?" said Kennie during a lull. "They are singing forward, round the galley fire. I've a good mind to go and join them; will you come? a second officer can do what a first can't."

"Yes, take your flute; that will be an excuse."

Given a trim ship and plenty of sea room, and it isn't all the wind that can blow that will succeed in lowering the spirits of the British sailor.

The jolliest of the crew of the *Brilliant* were seated to-night near the galley fire, or they clung to lockers or lay on the deck; it is all the same. It was cold enough to make a fire pleasant and agreeable, and they were all within speaking distance; they had pipes and tobacco and plates of sea-pie, for it was Friday night, the old custom of making Friday a kind of Banian day being still kept up in some vessels of the merchant service.

"Hullo! Mr McAlpine," cried the carpenter. "Right welcome, sir. And you too, Mr McCrane. Glad to see the smiling faces of the pair of you. Ain't we, mates?"

"That we are," and "that we be," came the ready chorus.

"Some sea-pie, gentlemen," said the cook, handing each a steaming basin of that most savoury dish.

"I made it," cried the bo'sun.

"Not all," cried another. "I rolled the paste."

"And I cut the beef."

"And I sliced the bacon."

"And I chopped the onions."

"And I pared the 'taters." This last from the cabin-boy.

"Ha! ha! ha!" roared the jolly carpenter. "I say, maties, blowed if we haven't all had a hand in the pie."

"Well, it is jolly eating anyhow," said Kenneth.

"The smell of it's enough to raise a dying man," quoth Archie.

"Bravo, sir," cried the bo'sun, "and I hopes it makes ye both 'appy."

"Happy, yes," said Kenneth. "I'm so happy now, I can sing and play."

"Oh! give us a toot on the old flute first."

Kenneth gave them "a toot."

"Now give us a song."

"Let the gentleman take his breath," the carpenter remonstrated.

"Never a breath," persisted the bo'sun. "He must pay his footin', I says. And I warrant you, too, he has as much pleasure in singing as we has in listenin' to 'im."

"Oh! shut up, old Barkshire," said somebody.

"Barkshire be bothered," cried the bo'sun. "I'm not ashamed to own my shire. You comes from the land o' *Tres* and *Pens*; you're west-country, you be. Have to fish for your breakfast every mornin', else ye doesn't get none: He! he!"

"Well, never mind," said the good-natured carpenter, smiling. "We're all nationalities here. Bill here is York; Tim is Irish; I'm just what Pipes calls me, Barkshire."

"And I and my friend are Scotch," said Kenneth.

"Hurrah! for a Scotch song, then."

It wasn't one, but several songs Kennie and Archie had to sing, but all Scotch, and what can beat them, reader mine?

> "Sing ony o' the auld Scotch sangs,
>   The blithesome or the sad;
> They mak' me laugh when I am wae,
>   And weep when I am glad.

> Though eyes grow dim and hair grow grey,
>   Until the day I dee,
> I'll bless the Scottish tongue that sings
>   The auld Scotch sangs to me."

There was no satisfying his audience, so once more Kennie had to fall back upon the flute. While playing, a heavy sea struck the vessel on the weather bow, and the water came tumbling down the hatchway; although it rushed forward among the men and hissed against the hot iron fending of the copper, they hardly shifted their positions.

But Kenneth played a selection of the best English, Irish, Scotch, and Welsh airs now, now merry, now plaintive and sad, now almost wailing, and anon merry again, once more.

There was a perfect chorus of applause when he had finished. The old bo'sun must crawl over to the corner where the musician was—although, owing to the motion of the ship, it was no easy task—and shake Kenneth by the hand.

"God bless you, young sir," he said, and the tears were in his eyes. "I was back in bonnie Berkshire all the time you was a-playin', sir. I saw my children, sir, runnin' among the daisies, the crimson poppies growin' among the corn's green, the waving lime trees all in flower and covered with bees—ah! sir, you took the old man home, you took him home."

"Don't talk twaddle," cried his tormentor; "he took us all home, for the matter o' that."

"A SHIP BORE DOWN AND TOOK US OFF."

"Sit down, ye ould fool!" cried Tim O'Flaherty.

Kenneth put up his flute, and the bo'sun sat down beside him.

"Hark to the thunder!" he said; "listen to the thud o' the seas. My eye! it is a night and a half. Just like the night we went over in the old *Salanella*."

"Went over!" cried the carpenter. "What d'ye mean?"

"Why, I means what I says, to be sure. We turned turtle. Every soul below was called to his account, and only myself and five more managed to cling to the keel."

"She must have been a barnacley old tub," said the cook, "else you wouldn't ha' got over the copper."

"You just mind your ladle, old man," said the carpenter. "You're only a cook, arter all, and Pipes knows what he's a-talking about."

"O' course I does," said Pipes. "Thank ye, Chips; it ain't very often you takes my part. O' course I knows what I'se a-talkin' about. The keel rolled over to us, and we easily got on top."

"Suffer much?"

Pipes did not look at the speaker, but away into vacancy as if he were recalling the past.

"Suffer!" he said. "I hope it may never be the lot o' anybody in this galley to know what we suffered. For three days and nights o' storm I and one other clung to that ship's bottom; the rest dropped off one by one or slipped willingly into the sea, glad to end their terrible misery.

"I never did think the ocean was so vast and empty-like till then, mates. All the weary days we did nothing but gaze and gaze around us, and hope and hope, and pray and pray. Well, blessed be His name, mates, God heard our prayers at last. A ship—'twas the second we'd seen, for the first took no notice of us—bore down and took us off, and that was no easy task in the condition our misery had reduced us to."

"Listen," cried one of the men.

There were three distinct knocks on the deck with a heavy boot; (A plan adopted in some merchant ships for calling the attention of those below to an order about to be given) then a stentorian voice sang down the hatchway,—

"All hands, shorten sail! Look alive there, lads. Tumble up. Tumble up."

A fiercer squall than any the vessel had yet encountered struck her before the men had time to reach the yards, and the sails they would have furled were rent into ribbons, and the noise they made as they fluttered out in the breeze was like the volley-firing of a company of soldiers. It was two hours before those whose watch was not on deck got back to the galley fire. It had just gone eight bells in the last dog watch, so the evening was still young.

Chapter Fifteen
Christmas Day in the Doldrums

"See the pudding, hear the fun;
The laugh and joke and glee;
The ship may in the Doldrums lie,
But—'tis Christmas Day at sea."

Anon.

Scene: A ship in the Doldrums. It is the saucy *Brilliant*. She has been to Calcutta, and is now on her way back to the Cape. And it is Christmas Day, and she ship is in the Doldrums. Longitude 90 degrees East; latitude nothing at all, for she is as nearly "on top o' the 'quator," as Jack calls it, as possible. She encountered a tornado farther north, which gives the reason for her being now somewhat out of her course. But she stood it well, and to see her now, with her long black lines, her tapering spars, and snow-white decks, you could not believe that but a fortnight before she had hardly a morsel of bulwark left, that, in fact, the bulwarks were more like sheep hurdles than anything shipshape.

The Doldrums! There isn't a breath of wind; the surface of the great rolling waves is as smooth as polished steel, and much about the same colour. The sun is beating straight down from a blue but cruelly hot sky. The pitch is soft in the deck seams; the men in the stoke-hole are to be pitied.

Yes, steam is up, there is a frothy wake behind her, and her bows cut through the water like a knife.

But the awning is spread all over the quarter-deck, and her tables are laid, for the captain is a right good fellow, and the men are all coming to dine with him.

They are dropping aft even now, one by one or twos and twos, somewhat shy-looking, but with beaming faces, and dressed in their best, bare-footed, in blue serge pants and clean spruce white jerseys.

"How different Christmas in the Doldrums is," said Captain Smith, "from what we are used to have it at home in old England. Sit in, men; no ceremony to-day. Mr McAlpine, you'll carve the beef. Mr McCrane, I'm sure you will show the men a good example at your end of the table. Now, doctor, will you ask a blessing?"

Fiddles were placed across the table—long sticks shipped together by pieces of line—and the cloth was laid over that, so that, in spite of the incessant and most uneasy motion of the vessel, the dishes themselves were kept fairly steady.

As soon as eating was well commenced, tongues were loosed, and the conversation flowed freely enough, and why should it not? The captain was jolly, frank, and open, and his officers gentlemen in manners, so the men were not afraid to speak before them.

Yarn followed yarn, and tale tale, but all short and crisp; the captain joked himself, and encouraged his men to joke, so that, despite the heat, it really was a very pleasant Christmas dinner-party.

But the coming of the pudding was the great event. For, you see, it was an immensely large one, and as the ship rolled so much, the danger of its being sent flying into the scuppers before reaching the table, and being all smashed, was very great indeed.

Even the night before, the captain had commissioned the doctor to superintend its safe delivery. And that worthy had positively got Chips to make a kind of ambulance stretcher, partly canvas and partly bamboo cane, to put the trencher on, and this was borne by two men.

"Now," said the captain, when the roast beef had been taken away, "are you all ready, doctor?"

"Yes," said the man of physic, wiping the sweat off his brow. "I'm all ready if the pudding is."

"The cook's waiting, sir," said the steward, who was trying to steady himself by keeping firm hold of the mizen rigging.

"Well, here's for off," said the surgeon, getting up.

"Do your duty like a man," cried the captain, laughing, as the doctor went staggering forward. "And keep to your legs, doctor, keep to your legs."

There was silence now around the table for many long anxious minutes.

It was a solemn time. There was nothing to be heard but the throb-throb of the engines—the beating of the ship's great heart.

Would the doctor and his party succeed in landing the pudding aft? That was the great question for the time being, which every one was asking himself. Would the pudding arrive in safety?

Every eye was turned forward.

Behold, they come. Their heads are already above the fore hatch. Slowly they emerge, and stand for a moment swaying hither and thither. The doctor heads the procession. The cook himself brings up the rear. Now the doctor's voice is heard.

"Are you all ready again, men?"

"All ready, sir."

"Steady, then; steady as you go. March!"

How steady they move! How quietly! A soldier's funeral is nothing to it! How they rock, and how they sway, taking advantage of every seeming break in the ship's motion, cautioning each other with uplifted fingers, the doctor with his left hand over the prize, the cook with his right, ready to clutch it if it moves, ready to fall with it if it falls.

Nearer and nearer they come. Nearer and nearer the great IT—the pudding—comes. And now it is almost alongside the captain and the expectant crew, when—oh moment of grief and horror!—the ship gives a fearful lurch, and the whole procession, pudding and all, is sent flying across the deck and brought up all of a heap close under the port bulwarks.

A groan of disappointment rises up from the table. The pudding is smashed to pieces, of course. No, for see—bravo! the doctor—he has clutched the trencher at a critical moment. Phoenix-like, he uprises with it from that chaos of arms and legs. He watches the chance. He gives one quick glance around him, at sea, at sky, at moving ship. He stakes his honour, his fame, and the very existence of that glorious globe of fragrant dough on one bold manoeuvre. Bearing it high over his head, he glides, he slides, he skates, one might say, towards the table; and in shorter time by far than it takes me to describe the gallant deed, he plumps the "great champion of the pudding race" down in front of the captain's pile of plates.

"Hurrah! hurrah!"

Why, the very sharks deep down in the ocean's blackest depths heard the shout; they took it for a battle-cry, and came surface-wards in all haste, making sure of a glorious feast. And an answering shout came up from the engine-room, where the stokers were at work. For they knew that the pudding was safely landed, and that their share would shortly come.

And the captain must needs shake the doctor by the hand, while tears of joy and admiration stood in his eyes.

"Doctor," he said, "you're a brick, sir, a brick and a half, sir. I never saw a bolder move. I never saw anything so pluckily done in my life before. I'm proud of my surgeon, proud of you."

Then he sat down.

The doctor made some reply, which was hardly heard amid the exclamations of accord in the captain's speech, which uprose from all round the table.

A rough old sea-dog of a doctor he was, too, a thorough sailor. Any one could have seen that at a glance. Rough he was, yet kindly-hearted, and there was not a man on board, from the captain to the Kroo boy who helped the cook, who wouldn't have risked his life for their surgeon.

I leave you to guess whether or not justice was done to that Christmas plum-pudding. Indeed, I only wish you could have seen the happy smiling faces that now surrounded the table, and really—though it was not polite of them—several of the crew had no less than *three* helps, for "Cut and come again" was the captain's motto on this Christmas Day in the Duldrums.

Well, of course songs and yarns followed dinner. The captain told a story, Archie told a story, Kenneth sang and played, the old bo'sun called Pipes had something queer to say, and so had the carpenter called Chips.

"Now then, doctor," cried the captain. "It's your turn. Tell us something good."

The doctor cleared his throat.

"I'll do my best, sir," said the doctor with a modest smile.

Chapter Sixteen
Frozen up in the North

"Now hie' we to the Norlan seas
And far-off fields of ice."

Anon.

"It is twenty years ago! Twenty years ago! Twenty years!" began the doctor.

"Yes, I own to it; no need for this matter-of-fact memory of mine to nudge me so, and keep on reminding me of the flight of sly old Father Time. 'Tis twenty years ago this very summer since I sailed away to Polar seas, in a small but sturdy brig of barely three hundred tons. A medical student I was, in charge of fifty men, all told, and with all a medical student's audacity and ignorance of the noble profession to which I have now the honour to belong. What cared I then if half the crew fell ill? There was plenty of medicine in the chest. I would do my best, and dose them. Well, if, after being dosed, they should die, why, the sea was deep enough—they should not want for decent burial! And what cared I that a fearful accident might take place, and heads be gashed, and limbs be crushed? There were surgical instruments *galore* on board, practice makes perfect, and if my patients succumbed after an operation, well, every dog has his day, and the *post hoc propter hoc* argument has been proved to be unsound.

"Gentlemen, have ever you roughed it in the Arctic Ocean, in a bit of a ship so small that a schoolboy, with average length of legs, could clear its decks from binnacle to bowsprit with a hop, step, and jump, the saloon not larger than two railway compartments, your state-room not half so big as one? Have you been in a gale of wind in such a craft? Was she on her beam-ends, with the cold, green seas, curling higher and higher as they advanced, forming awful arches of water, into which the vessel seemed to be sucked, and which broke, not *on*, but over and beyond her? Have you been ice-logged in a sea-way in such a vessel, no land, nor even a berg, in sight — only the restless waves, that twanged and hummed, and sang in the frosty air as they passed you, with bows and bulwarks, decks and spars, and rigging and blocks, mere shapes of ice, and ice alone to all appearance, the men's caps and coats, and hair and beards, so white with the freezing spray, that they looked, as they moved to and fro on the slippery decks, like the ghostly crew of a ghost ship? Have you been in such a craft when she was being squeezed in this pack, the one dark spot in the midst of a limitless plain of dazzling snow-clad ice, all lifting and rolling and moving with the pressure of the invisible waves that are passing swiftly underneath? Have you ever heard the terrible sounds an ice-pack emits, when the swell from a distant storm comes sweeping under it, the groaning, the wailing, grinding, griding noise, as if the ocean on which you stood were filled with old-world monsters in their dying agonies? Have you ever listened to the roaring thunder of a lofty iceberg rent in pieces, and falling headlong into the sea? Have you stood on the pack and seen two bergs crush an acre of bay ice between them, piling the pieces one over the other, like leaves of a book or cards in a pack, till they stood high as the tallest tree in a forest of pines? Have you been out alone on the ice-field at night, far away from your ship, amid a silence that, like Egyptian darkness, could be felt, watching the glorious tints of the —

ON THE BORDERS OF ETERNAL ICE.

> "'Aurora Borealis race,
> That flit ere you can point their place?'

"And, even while gazing and admiring, have you seen dark clouds roll rapidly up from the horizon and blot this aurora out, so that ere you could reach your brig you were surrounded by swirling drift and blinding snow, more dangerous far than the sand-storms that sweep over the Soudan deserts, with the thunder rattling close o'erhead, and the bewildering lightning in swift diffusive gleams intensifying the cave-like darkness that followed?

"If such experiences have not been yours, you may have been tossed about on the giant waves of the broad Atlantic, you may have weathered the Cape in a gale, and the Horn in a snow-storm, you may have sweltered for weeks in a rolling calm under a tropical sun, and been the sport of a tornado in the Indian Ocean, yet there are wonders in the mighty deep seen by some who go down to the sea in ships to which you are a total stranger. From beginning to end, our voyage in that little brig, twenty years ago, was a non-propitious one. We ran before a gale all the way to Lerwick, where the Greenland fleet lay anchored. We had hardly left the rock-bound shores of Shetland—that 'sea-begirdled peat moss'—ere the blackness of darkness settled down on the ocean around us; and storm and tempest became our constant companions for three long weeks, till sheltered at last under the lee of the pack, with bowsprit and topmasts gone, and the bulwarks more like the palings one sometimes sees around a cattle-field than anything else in the world. But even worse was to follow: with several other ships we took the ice, which was loose, and in three weeks' time we found ourselves all alone in the midst of a hard frozen ice-field, and fully one hundred miles from the open water, a bright blue frosty sky above us, and in silence—a silence never broken even by the cry of a bird or guttural roar of Arctic bear.

"After many months of 'solitary confinement,' we escaped and reached home at last. Many of the men's relations met us on the pier, dressed in deepest mourning; the 'blacks,' as such dress is called, had been donned for us, for our ship had been reported as lost with all hands!

"Life in that lonesome ice-pack was a weary 'bide,'—

> "'Day after day, day after day,
> And neither breath nor motion.'

"No, not as much wind as would have sufficed to lift a snowflake, never a cloud in the sky, and the sun going round and round and round, but far above the horizon even at midnight. We tired of reading books; we tired of card-playing and games on the ice; we even tired of music itself. Monotony generated *ennui*; *ennui* bred melancholy; plenty of exercise on the ice alone could save us from succumbing to actual illness. We knew that well, but we were thoroughly apathetic, and did not care to take it. The captain, a young and energetic man, at last hit upon a happy expedient which succeeded most completely in restoring something of life and animation to the crew, who were rapidly merging into a state of Rip Van Winkleism, painful to behold. He determined to form a camp three miles away from the ship. Simply walking to and from it would be some little excitement, it would be exercise with a purpose, and exercise, as medical men will tell you, without pleasure or purpose, is entirely useless in a hygienic point of view.

"Our captain, the first and second mates, and myself were seated at breakfast one morning when he made his proposal.

THE KING OF THE POLAR SEA.

"'Doctor,' he said—NB, he called me 'Doctor' always, but at that time I had no more business with the title than the tailor had—

"'Doctor, how are the men getting on forward?'

"'They haven't much life in them,' I replied; 'they are all making silver rings now out of sixpenny bits and shillings. That is the latest fad, but the coins will soon be all used up; then I suppose all hands will go to sleep for a month or two.'

"'I think, doctor,' said Captain Peters, 'that their livers want stirring up. Eh? Don't you, doctor?'

"'Well,' I replied, 'anything for a quiet life. There is plenty of blue pill and black draught on board. I'll stir their livers up. Pass the ham.'

"'All right, then,' said the captain; 'you stir their livers up, and I'll propose something to-morrow to prevent them getting sluggish again.'

"True to my promise, I gave all hands a blue pill that night, and next forenoon, at a little before twelve, the captain called the men aft, and ordered the steward to bring up a gallon of rum and five pounds of tobacco. Then he doled out the latter and ordered the mainbrace to be spliced. The men after this looked more lively than they had done for a month.

"'Now that I've got you awake with the help of the doctor and black Jack' (black Jack was the rum measure), said the captain, 'let me tell you what we are going to do. We are going to convey wood and canvas by sleigh across the pack, to a patch of bay ice about three miles from here, and by the side of it, on the top of the heavy berg, we will build a tent, with a fire-place in it, big enough to roast a bear. This tent or marquee will be a regular Hall of Delights by the sad sea wave; we will cook in it, and eat in it, and dance and sing and tell stories in it. What say you, men?'

"The men broke out into a wild cheer.

"'Wait a wee,' continued the captain; 'I'm going to do more for you than that, for goodness only knows how long we may have to remain in this gloomy ice-field, and if I don't keep you alive, you'll all go to sleep and not waken any more in this world. We shall set to work, then, and make an immense great hole in that patch of bay ice, and it will be your duty to keep it from freezing; then seals will come up, and maybe walruses too, and catching these and the sharks will be glorious fun and keep us all alive and awake. That is my plan complete.'

"This idea of the captain's was a splendid one, and we all entered into it heart and soul. We built rude sledges and tooled wood and all other necessaries over the pack, and before a week was over we had erected a large and handsome marquee with a floor of timber, doors and windows, table and fire-place all comfortable and jolly.

"We had hammocks slung round it also, so that when tired we could lounge and read, or lounge and sleep, and on the whole we felt like new beings, and each of us was as happy as a schoolboy with a tin whistle.

"The opening in the bay ice proved a wondrous success, for the rays of sunlight penetrated far down into the black-blue water, and seals, seeing the light from afar, swam wondering towards it, then finding a hole, came out to breathe and look about them, and so fell victims to their curiosity. We had seal's liver and bacon for breakfast then, and found it a great treat. We skinned the phocas for sake of their blubber, with the following results: sharks in dozens came to eat the crangs we threw back into the sea, and birds reappeared, malleys, gulls, skuas, and terns, to pick up the stray bits of grease, so we had sport enough, and regained our spirits and strength in consequence. But when a great fire was built on a berg, and the carcase of a seal roasted thereon, bears sniffed the perfume, though they must have been miles and miles away, and came prowling down to the feast, which I ought to add had been prepared for their especial delectation.

IN QUEST OF GAME.

"They were somewhat shy at first, they preferred squatting at a distance, and contenting themselves with the delicious odour of the tit-bits placed temptingly on the hummock near, but as their numbers increased, so did their courage, and before very long we had the satisfaction of seeing them in twos and even threes, wrangling together over juicy joints. Then was our chance, and we did not hesitate to avail ourselves thereof. Hungry bears are by no means easily scared, and so our sport was good.

"There was no more laziness among our crew now, no more danger of our fellows falling into Rip Van Winkleism, for every day brought us sport and excitement and fun and adventure. We all began to sing again, and that is always a good sign on board a ship. There was singing fore and singing aft, and tales told in the saloon and yarns spun around the galley fire.

"The Hall of Delights by the sad sea wave proved a very great success indeed. Somehow or other we came to like it better than the ship itself, and although we always came home to sleep, it was often very late indeed before we scrambled on board our slippery-decked brig, and went below to the dingy darkness of state-room, hammock, or bunk.

"In this Hall of Delights we had music, for Peter Kelty played the violin, and Sandy Watson the clarionet; then there was big Magnus Rugg could put in a bass with his voice alone that you couldn't have told from a violoncello. We had plenty of fire in the hall, but when the fiddles started of an evening, it wasn't much heat we needed, for those—

"'Hornpipes, jigs, strathspeys, and reels,
Put life and mettle in our heels.'

"When tired of dancing, or rather, I should say, in the intervals between the dances, we had singing and recitations. The simplest of the simple both were, for in the latter I don't think we ever got beyond 'Douglas's Tragedy' or 'Tam o' Shanter,' and in the former 'Annie Laurie' or 'The Braes o' Balquidder' were far more appreciated than anything from the best of operas could have been.

"But the *summus mons*, in a musical way, was attained by our spectioneer, or third officer, for he not only sang most charmingly, but he accompanied himself on the zither.

"He was somewhat of a character, was this individual. He was far from old-looking in the face, but his hair and beard were like the very snow itself. He seldom even smiled, or if he did, it was a languid, sad kind of smile that kept well down about the lips, and never curved round the eyes or made them sparkle. He was tender and kind in heart, though, and a favourite with all hands.

"By-the-bye, his name was Summers, but he was always called Winter, and didn't mind it a bit, he was so good-natured.

"We were all enjoying ourselves one evening in the Hall of Delights, we had danced till the fiddlers were tired, and everybody that could sing had sung, so there was a kind of lull—a momentary silence, in fact. Now, as it was nearly ten o'clock, if this silence had continued for even fifteen seconds, the captain would certainly have jumped up and said:

"'Well, lads, we'd better be moving.'

"We didn't feel like moving yet, so the silence was not allowed to extend itself.

"'Hi!' cried Kelty, 'I call upon you for a *comic* song, Mr Winter.'

"'Or a *funny* story,' cried somebody else.

"There was loud laughing at the bare idea of Winter treating us to either.

"Winter looked round among us, in an amused kind of way, as if he quite enjoyed the joke, and when the laugh subsided, we all glanced towards him for his reply. I think I see him now; one hand rested on the zither bringing out stray chords, the other rested on the table, the great oil lamp that stood at one side threw his features into semi-shadow, and there was a thoughtful far-away look in his eyes.

"'Yes,' he said, at last, 'I'll tell you a story.'

"'A funny one? Eh?' said the mate.

"'Well—no, not *very* funny. But anything to pass the time, I suppose. I'll tell you a story of my own grey hairs.'

"'Capital,' we cried, and hammered with our feet on the wooden floor, by way of giving him encouragement. Then we lit our pipes and prepared to listen."

Chapter Seventeen
A Tale Told on the Sea of Ice

"The mariner whose eye is bright,
Whose beard with age is hoar."

Coleridge.

Scene: The good ship *Brilliant* in the Doldrums. Crew at their Christmas dinner. The doctor continues his story.

"'In the year 18—, I sailed from Hull in the good barque *Constance*, bound for Jan Mayen and Spitzbergen, in pursuit of seals and walruses. I was a very young man then, and, indeed, white though my hair be and snowy my beard, I am not old yet. It is not age that has made me grey, but grief, and one of the most terrible experiences it has probably ever been the lot of man to undergo.

"'Our voyage to the Arctic seas was a pleasant enough one. We did not encounter a single gale, and we made the country in less than a fortnight. We met the seals a little north of Mount Beerenberg, coming southward to the low pack ice in thousands; nay, but in millions; for the sea was black with their beautiful heads for miles on each side of our ship, and as far north as we could see from the masthead. Oh, didn't our hearts beat high then! We saw fortune within our reach, and had bright visions of a splendid voyage, a ship full to the hatches, with bings of skins on deck, and an early return to sunny England, our sweethearts and wives. We put about and followed the seals, and ere many days were past had the satisfaction of seeing them take the ice. There would soon be enough to fill all the ships in the Greenland fleet. We had but to wait a week or two until the young were big enough to capture. What a happy crew we were now! It was singing forward and laughing aft, all day long. But alas! and alas! for the fickleness of fortune, a wretched, greedy old Dutch ship came in, and no sooner saw the seals on the ice than she lowered her boats, and in spite of our remonstrances, proceeded to the ice. Twenty-four hours afterwards there was not one single seal, of all the myriads that had taken the ice, visible anywhere, above or below—the Dutch boats had scared them all away. It was all our captain and myself—I had only that spring got my certificate as mate—could do to prevent our men from boarding the Dutchman, and taking summary vengeance on that idiot skipper and his idiot crew.

"'We got up sail as soon as possible, and began forging through the loose pack ice, in the hope of again falling in with fortune in the shape of seals. We did sight them far in towards the west, and on heavier ice than we generally cared to venture among; but we did not think twice about the matter then. We worked our vessel in, and in, and in, towards our game, when the wind failed us all at once, and every seal disappeared as if by magic, or as if they had been but phantoms of the brain. To add to our grief, hard frost set in, and lasted for many weeks. We hoped against hope we would get clear before long, and still be in time to follow the old seals northwards toward Spitzbergen. So we dreamt. Well, clouds banked up on the southern horizon at last, and snow fell, such snow as I had never seen before, and have seen but once or twice since. Every flake was as big as a hand. In less than twelve hours the whole of that vast ice-pack was one level surface, one unbroken field of dazzling snow. But then came the wind—a fierce and fearful gale—and the bergs rose and fell around us and tossed and tumbled, as if we had been in the middle of a troubled sea, the waves of which were walls of snow. Our barque was heaved up, now forward, now aft, and ground and torn, till we could hear the very timbers cracking and rending beneath us, and we knew then she was doomed—knew that when the ice that nipped her receded, and the pressure abated, she would sink. This happened sooner far than we could have believed possible. While the wind still roared through the rigging, and all between decks was as dark as a winter midnight with the clouds of drifting, driving snow, suddenly the sides of the saloon, in which the captain, myself, and the other mate were sitting, came crashing and splintering in upon us, and we had barely time to spring to the companion ladder before the freer ice was grinding amid a chaos of broken boards and timbers in the very place where we had been sitting barely three seconds before. Almost at the same moment the after-part of the ship took fire.

"'How this happened I cannot tell. Friction itself would fire the rum, or the blazing coals from the broken stove might have been thrown among the staved casks. Explosion after explosion occurred; then the water rushed forward, and the vessel began at once to be sucked under. We had barely a quarter of an hour to clear out, but even in that short time we managed to land three boats with blankets and provisions on the ice, and this, too, in spite of the storm, in spite of the numbing wind, and the drifting, choking, powdery snow.

"'We huddled together beneath the boats for hours and hours, and when the wind went down at last, we crawled out—those who could crawl—the living from among the dead, the maimed and sick. Out of a crew of thirty-nine only twenty-four answered to their names the morning after the wreck of the good barque *Constance*. We sunk the dead between the bergs, and waited for others to die—waited days and days; then the remainder of us started southwards with two of the whalers to seek for the open water. The frost had set in again harder than ever, and the sun was very bright, but it was a terrible journey, nevertheless, and five more of us, including our captain, succumbed to cold and hardship before we stood at last on the edge of the solid pack with the open water all before us.

"'Ay, there it was—the open water, the Southern Sea—black as ink in the foreground, blue beyond, and dotted here and there with little floating bergs, just as the sky above was flecked with little fleecy, floating clouds. And we knew well that hundreds of miles beneath the horizon lay Iceland, the country we must try to reach, even if we perished in the attempt.

"'We launched our boats and grasped our oars, and so began our long and dangerous voyage. Provisions we had, and compasses; water we had none, but we took on board huge pieces of fresh-water ice that we were lucky enough to find on top of the salt sea bergs.

"'All went well for days and days, and, much to our joy, a breeze sprang up. The sail was set. We were so far south now that, summer though it was, the sun set; then we steered by the stars, for as yet clouds had not obscured the sky. I had command of our boat; the steward had charge of the other.

"'One morning I was saddened to see a body launched overboard from our companion boat, which was a little way ahead at the time. As we sailed up I had just time to notice it was the steward himself ere a terrible specimen of the hammer-headed shark sprang, monster-like, out of the sea, and next moment the body had disappeared.

"'The rugged mountain peaks of Iceland at last! With what joy we hailed them, only those who have been so situated can understand or appreciate. Yes, the mountains were very rugged, very much peaked and jagged, but we knew that in the freer glens betwixt them, and at the head waters of many a lonely fiord, dwelt a rude but kindly-hearted people, who would gladly welcome and shelter the shipwrecked mariners.

"'And in two days at the furthest our trials would be over; so we fondly imagined. Alas! they were but beginning. In a few hours after we had sighted the distant hills the wind completely failed us, while up from the south came, rolling and tumbling along the surface of the ocean, a bank of dark fog, and we were soon completely enveloped. We called to the other boat to keep near us, and trusting now entirely to our compasses, we took to our oars once more.

"'For half a day our boats kept together, but as soon as night and darkness fell, the wind got up, and the sea became rough, dashing continually on board of us, and necessitating constant work in baling. Towards morning the wind had increased to a gale, and we were running before it under our small, closely reefed mainsail and a trifle of jib. Where we were running we knew not, and, I think, hardly cared. We were completely exhausted with the wet and the cold. Our ice and the provisions were gone, and even the compass lost.

"'The sun broke through the fog at last, and to some extent the wind abated, but the sea still ran houses high. I looked up from the place where I sat, mechanically grasping the tiller. Heavens! what a sight I witnessed! When night had come on, we had been seven in our boat; now we were but three, that is two more than myself. Of the others two had leapt overboard mad, or been washed away; two sat alive but pale and ghastly, grasping in white-blue hands, that I could see were sadly frost-bitten, the icy sheets of the sails. One poor fellow was curled up dead under the bows; the other had fallen backwards over a thwart as if he had caught a crab, and there he lay with his long yellow hair floating in the water with which the boat was half full, and his sightless eyes turned sunwards.

"The life still there upon his hair,
The death within his eyes."

"Bale, men, bale the boat," I cried, "bale her, or we shall sink."

"'They turned their awful cadaverous faces towards me, they opened their mouths as if to speak, but a sound 'twixt a moan and a gurgle was all that came from their throats; then they lifted their hands and tapped the backs of their fingers against the gunwale of the boat, and they rattled as if they had been made of wood, so sorely were they frozen.

"'Many, many times during that long and dreadful day did those two poor fellows turn towards me, and they kept signing, signing to me for the help they were pleading for in vain, and ever from their throats came that awful gurgling moan. Oh! men, I think I see and hear them now.

"'Night fell at last, night and pitchy darkness, and next morning I was alone on the sea. Alone with the dead!

"'And all that day I sat there, as if in the power of some strange nightmare. The use of every limb I retained as well as that of head and body, but still I did not or could not move, but I kept praying, praying not for the cold and icy wind to fall, not for the clouds and fog to roll away, or the sea to go down, but praying for death, a share of the death I saw around me.

"'Towards the afternoon I think I must have slept or fallen into a kind of a trance. The wind had quite gone down when I again recovered a sort of consciousness. There was no more broken water, but a heavy tumbling swell on the eastward when I looked. These huge heaving smooth waves seemed to take on the appearance of monsters of the deep, raising their awful heads and backs, grim and grey and cold, above the sea; but westward they were moving masses crimson and black. The sky was a wonderful sight. From the sun's upper limit to the zenith it was hung with curtains of blue-grey clouds, one behind the other, as it were, the edges all zig-zagged and fringed with red. All round the sun itself was a coppery haze. To the north the sky was clear and of a bright lemon yellow; to the east it was clear also, and *green*.

"'I sat gazing at clouds, and sky till they faded into the gloom of night; they got thinner and thinner then, and stars shone through them, and soon they vanished entirely, and the stars had it all their own way.

"'I felt no hunger, no thirst, no pain, no pleasure; my condition was one of pure apathy; my very soul appeared dead within me.

"'Soon a bright light shone out of the north with tints of carmine, pale yellow, and green; it was the aurora, and long fringes of pale phosphorescent light descended from the sky overhead. I could have touched them with my hand had they been tangible. They were independent of the far-off aurora. They assumed the forms of gigantic fern leaves and danced dazzlingly before my eyes, and I could almost imagine they emitted a hissing, crackling sound.

"'Then my brain began to reel, and I fell forward in the boat among my dead companions.

"'A shock awoke me at last. Cold and shivering now, I sat up and rubbed my eyes. Morning was breaking gloomy and grey over the sea, and some gulls were wheeling and screaming about in the air.

"'Once again the shock, and the boat trembled from stem to stern, and some birds rose up out of the bows and floated slowly away. They had been gorging on the dead.

"'The shocks to the boat were easily accounted for: the sea was alive with monster sharks.

"'O God! men, it was a fearful sight. There was something appalling and horrible in the very way they *gambolled* around the boat. Their eyes told me one thing: they had come for the dead—and the living.

"'I cannot tell you whether I really did lift the bodies of my late companions and throw them overboard. I would even now fain believe this was but a dream. If so, it was terribly real, the fighting, wrangling sharks in the sea, the birds wheeling and screaming above.

"'My boat was picked up that day by some Icelandic fisherman; there was no one in it but myself, men, white in hair, white in beard, as you now behold me.'"

So ended the spectioneer's story, and so ended that Christmas dinner in the Doldrums, but both Kenneth and Archie long, long after this used to speak about it amid other scenes and in other climes, and both agreed it was one of the pleasantest afternoons ever they had spent in life.

The two friends made many a voyage together in the *Brilliant*, and together came through no little adventure, and saw many a strange sight in many a strange sea. They came to love the vessel at last, for real sailors do love their ships. They loved her and called her the saucy *Brilliant*, and the dear old ship, and quite a host of other pet names.

"But alas! and alas?" said Kenneth to Archie one day, while they stood together on the quarter-deck, "we are not making our fortunes. We will never get rich at sea. And by-and-bye, you know, we'll be getting fearfully old."

"Yes," said Archie, "I'm feeling old already. We are both of us over twenty."

"Sad thought! yes?" added Kenneth. "So I propose we leave the dear old stupid craft at the end of this voyage, Archie."

And so they did, reader. And thus our tale runs on, but the scenes must change.

End of Book Two.

Chapter Eighteen
On the Unknown River

"Most glorious night,
Thou wert not sent for slumber! let me be
A sharer in thy fierce and fair delight."

Byron.

Scene: Night on an unknown river, which, dark and deep and sluggish, is rolling onwards to the distant ocean through a wild and beautiful district in the interior, nay, but ill the very centre of Africa. The centre it may well be called, for it is near the equator, and hundreds of miles from the Indian Ocean. Night on the river, but not darkness. A round moon has risen, the clouds, dazzled by its splendour, have parted to let it pass; its light is flooding hill and dell and forest, and changing the river itself to—apparently—a moving flood of molten gold.

Light, but not darkness. Night, but not silence either. Were it possible for any one to pass swiftly and unseen along the banks of the unknown river at such an hour and on such a night as this, what sights he would see, what sounds would fall upon his listening ear! Come with me in imagination! Take heed of those rocks; they are slippery at the edge, for the rainy season is not yet past. To fall into the stream would mean an ugly death, were you even as good a swimmer as the gallant Webb. There are no signs of life in the water, it is true, but the plash of your fall would raise a score of awful heads above it; the crocodiles would be upon you with lightning speed, and rend you from limb to limb.

Peer over the cliff just there. What is that lying on the mud close by the river? Is it the trunk of some dead tree? Drop a pebble on it. See; it moves off into the river and slowly disappears—a crocodile.

Hark to that horrible sound! it makes the very "welkin" ring,—a loud, discordant, coughing, bellowing roar. It is the lion-king of the forest. He loves not the moonlight. It baulks him of his prey; so there is anger in that growl. But you hardly can tell whence it comes; at one moment, it sounds over yonder among the rocks, next, down in that lonesome ravine, and next, in the forest behind you.

Look at those great birds. They fly so closely over our heads that their mighty wings overshadow us for a moment, and we can hear the rustling, creaking sound made by their feathers. There is something lying dead in the valley beyond the hill, and these are vultures going to gorge by the moonlight.

Two great necks are raised like poles behind a rock as the birds fly in that direction. Giraffes, who have been sleeping—there in the open, their heads leaning on the rocks, their ears doing duty even in slumber, but ready if danger draws near to—

"Burst like whirlwind o'er the waste,
To thunder o'er the plain."

In yonder, beneath that flowery, ferny bank, is the leopard's cave—the tiger cat. If you went near enough you would see her fiery eyes, and hear a low, ominous growl that would chill you to the spine.

Kenneth Mcalpine

Yes, wild beasts and wild birds keep close to-night; for a little while only; when the deer and the antelope steal down to the river, they will come forth, and there will be yells and shrieks of anger, pain, and terror, and an awful feast to follow.

Behold those lordly elephants; how they trumpet and roar! They are excited about something.

Something unusual has happened, or they would not be there at this hour. Ha! There is a boat on the river, creeping up under the shadow of the rocks. What mystery is this? There are white men in it, too, and right merrily they are paddling along. But never before have the waters of this unknown river been stirred by oar of European.

For not only is the country all around here a wild one, but it has the name, at all events, of being inhabited by a race of savages that are never at peace, who are born, live, and die on the war-path—the Logobo men.

"Couldn't we go a little nearer?" said Harvey, who sat in the stern sheets near the tall Arab Zona, who was steering, Kenneth and Archie having an oar each.

"Couldn't we go a little nearer and have a shot at that elephant?"

"No, no, no," cried Zona, hastily; "we must keep in the shade, gentlemen. Even the moon is not our friend, pleasant though her light be. But the sound of your rifle would raise the Logobo men, and a thousand poisoned arrows would soon be whistling round our heads. We could not escape."

"Before morning," said Kenneth, "according to your reckoning, my good Zona, we should be well through the Logobo country, and among friends?"

"True," replied Zona; "we will be among friends all the way to the land of gold, I trust."

"The land of gold!" exclaimed Kenneth; "what a fascinating phrase! Zona, when we met you in Zanzibar our lucky stars must have been in the ascendant."

Zona gave a little laugh.

"It is the land of gold," he said, "that we are going to, it is true; but no man that ever yet tried brought that gold down to the coast."

"And why, my friend?"

"Why? I cannot tell you all the reasons why. They say the gold is guarded by evil spirits, that the hills where it is to be found are encircled by giant forests, by terrible swamps, the breath of which is more feared by the Arab than spear of savage foeman."

"We can but try," said Kenneth.

"Zona," said Archie, "did ever you hear the line of that old song, 'The March of the Cameron Men,' which says, 'Whatever a man dares he can do'?"

"Gentlemen all," replied Zona, "the Arab is the most daring of all men who live; the Arab has sought this gold that we are going in quest of; the Arab has failed! I have spoken."

"Worthy Zona," said Harvey, laughing, "you have an excellent opinion of your people, and an excellent opinion of yourself. Nay, never start, man. I love you for it. But let me tell you this. There is one thing in which even an Arab gold-seeker, with all his pluck and daring, may fail in—"

"And that is?" said Zona.

"Knowledge of prospecting."

"I am in the dark as to your meaning," said Zona.

"I know you are, and so are all your people. In other words, then, they don't know where to look for the gold. Now listen, friend. I have spent years and years in the gold regions of California—"

"I say, Harvey, old man," said Kenneth, "you weren't much the better of it. Eh?"

"True," replied Harvey, with a sigh; "else you wouldn't have found me working as an ordinary seaman before the mast in a craft like the *Brilliant*."

"Forgive me," said Kenneth, stretching out his hand, which Harvey readily grasped. "Forgive me; I didn't mean to hurt your feelings. I found you before the mast, it is true; but I took to you from the first hour we met. You have got the grit of a good man in you. Else Archie and I wouldn't have asked you to come with us on this gold-hunt, which after all may turn out to be a wild-goose chase."

"But it will *not* be a wild-goose chase. Man, I tell you this, the very mud of the river we are now floating over contains gold dust. We are going to trace that gold to its source, and find it in nuggets."

"I have found gold before," he continued. "I have made two fortunes and lost them, worse luck; but I can tell you whether or not gold lies in any country, if I get but one glance at the land, or but walk over it once. Fear not then, I won't deceive you, nor myself."

"Well, we shall trust to your skill," said Archie.

"And to Zona's," added Kenneth.

"To Zona's, certainly."

Let us hark back, reader, in our tale for a moment, and explain the appearance of our adventurers on this wild dark river of Africa at such a time of night.

The *Brilliant* then was in the habit of touching occasionally at Zanzibar in her passage from the East Indies to the Cape. Being much on shore, Kenneth could not help becoming acquainted with some of the numerous Portuguese merchants, who had settled in that strange city,—if a Portuguese merchant can be said to settle anywhere, for they are, like ourselves, a nation of wanderers. They are hospitable at their houses, however, and Kenneth and Archie too were made welcome, enough, and many a quiet cup of coffee they drank in the cool of the evening on great square housetops overlooking the blue sea.

They would sit far into the night, listening to stories of the interior of Africa, of wild adventures with wild beasts and wilder men, of great forest land and terrible swamps, of the country of the dwarfs and the dreaded gorilla, and of diamond caves, and caves in which nuggets of the richest gold were to be had for the gathering.

No wonder that such stories as these fired the young blood of our heroes Kenneth and Archie. They both longed to be rich; it was no mean ambition, for riches would be valued by neither as a mere hoard of wealth, but for the good they could accomplish therewith in the dear wild land of their nativity.

"Oh!" said Kenneth one evening as he sat on a roof-top under the quiet stars, listening to the conversation of his friend Morosco. "Oh! if I could but get up and command an expedition into the interior!"

"Ha! ha!" laughed the Portuguese, "an idle dream. Ten thousand men could not penetrate into the land of gold and diamonds."

"But," said Archie, "two or three might."

"Ah!" cried Morosco, "there you have it, young sir; one man may do more in Africa than an army. It has ever been thus; look at your Livingstone for example."

Then Kenneth took to thinking, and for days said no more on the subject even to Archie. But one evening, he asked him to come for a row among the coral islands. It was nearly sundown. There was not a ripple on the water, only a yellow haze all along the horizon, with the broad sun sinking red through it.

Kenneth lay on his oars, and let the boat float wherever the tide cared to take her.

"What a lovely night, Archie!" said Kenneth at last. "What a lovely colour is in the sky! The clouds are gold, the sea is gold, the consuls' houses and the sultan's palace are roofed in gold, the lofty palm-trees are tipped with gold, and the waves are rippling and lisping on sands of gold."

"Ah!" replied Archie, "my dear brother, your thoughts are steeped in gold. Morosco's stories have given you gold fever—but there, I won't laugh at you, for I tell you I know all your longings, and I, too, have the same."

Kenneth stretched across the thwarts and pressed his friend's hand.

"You'll go," he said, "you'll come with me into the interior. You'll brave danger? Everything?"

"Everything," replied Archie. "We are young, strong, healthy, hearty; why should we not? But," he continued, "while you have been dreaming I have been scheming. Zona, an Arab friend of mine, and a soldier, has been on expeditions into and beyond the Logobo country already; I have spoken to him, he is willing to venture with us. And so will Harvey."

THE SLAVE-BOY'S DREAM OF HOME.

"Harvey?" said Kenneth.

"Yes, he is like ourselves, a Scot. He will, he says, do or dare anything for a change."

"Hurrah!" cried Kenneth.

He was so excited now that he must needs bend to his oars again, and the light skiff in which he rowed seemed actually to skim the water like a skipjack. For his actions were keeping pace with his thoughts. And all the way down to the Cape, in what was to be their last voyage in the *Brilliant*, there was little else talked about by the three friends but their coming adventures in the land of gold.

When paid off, they took passage, for cheapness' sake, in an Arab dhow to Zanzibar. It was a long voyage in such a craft, and a rough one in many ways, for they got little to eat except dates and rice. But what cared they? The rice, in their eyes, seemed like little nuggets of gold. They reached Zanzibar safe and sound, and made haste to see Zona, the Arab chief, and arrange everything.

Zona brought with him a bold but honest-looking black boy. He was to be their guide through the country beyond Logobo. This boy, called Essequibo, came from there. Nay, let me rather say had been dragged from there by cruel and heartless slave-dealers.

Though an Arab, Zona had a good heart. He had first seen little Essequibo asleep on the rude steps of the slave auction mart at Lamoo, and his soul warmed to the poor lad. Dreaming the boy was of his far-off home in the interior, of the little village among the cocoa palms, where his mother and father lived ere that terrible night when the Arabs fell on them with chains and fire,—fire for the town, chains for the captives. Dreaming of home, dreaming that he was back once more, roaming with his brothers and sisters in the free forest, through the jungle, over hills purple with glorious heaths, through woods dark even at midday, or by the lakes where the hippopotami bathe and wallow, and where under the pale rays of the moon the deer and hart steal down to drink, their every movement watched by the wary leopard.

Though but a child when stolen from his home, and at the time of our tale in his fifteenth year, Essequibo had not forgotten a single hill or dale or creek or even tree of his native country. He was bold, bright, and faithful, as will be seen.

The preparations for the great journey had been very simple, perhaps too much so, for they consisted mainly in arms and ammunition. Kenneth, with all the simple faith of his countrymen, had put Nannie's old Bible in his wallet. In his wallet, too, Archie had slyly deposited the flute.

"An old Scotch air," he had said, "may help to 'liven us up when things look black and drear."

They had travelled thus far almost without adventure. They were now in the very heart of the warlike Logobos, but as yet had seen nothing more terrible than the denizens of forests and river I have already described.

Chapter Nineteen
The Search for the Land of Gold

Scene:—Daybreak on the unknown river. The stream is a good mile wide here; its banks are lined with a cloudland of green, the great trees trailing their branches in the water. A sand bar at one side, jutting far out into the river, tall crimson ibises standing thereon like a regiment of British soldiers. The mist of morning uprising everywhere off the woods and off the water. One long red cloud in the east heralding the approach of the god of day. Silence over all, except for the dip of the oars—they are muffled—as our adventurers' boat rapidly nears the shore to seek the friendly shelter of the tree-fringe.

"So far on our way, thank heaven," said Kenneth, as soon as the boat was hidden and the party had landed on a little bank deeply bedded with brown leaves.

"So far, and now for breakfast."

Yes, now for breakfast, reader, and a very frugal one it was; some handfuls of boiled rice and a morsel of biscuit steeped in the water to make it go down.

This had been their fare for days and days, but added thereto was the fruit that Essequibo never failed to find.

Fish there were in this great river in abundance, fish that they had plenty of means of catching too, but none of cooking without danger; for smoke might betray their presence to an enemy more implacable and merciless than the wildest beast in the jungle.

The long hot day passed drearily away. They sat or reclined mostly in a circle, carrying on a conversation in voices but little over a whisper.

When the day was at its very hottest, when there was not a leaf stirring in the branches above, when the monkeys that more than once had visited them, creeping nearer and nearer with curious half-frightened gaze, had sought the darkest, coolest nooks of the forest, and the—

"Strange bright birds on starry wing—"

had ceased their low plaintive songs, and sat open-mouthed and all a-gasp on the boughs, then sleep stole over every one, and it was far into the afternoon ere they awoke.

The sun went down at last, and darkness—a tropical darkness—very soon followed. Lights might now be seen flitting about among the trees; the fire-flies and curious creeping things went gliding hither and thither on the ground, all ablaze with phosphorescent light. Yonder knobs of fire that jump about so mysteriously are beetles; that long line of fire wriggling snake-like at the tree foot is the dreaded brown centipede, whose bite is death.

They must not leave their hiding-place yet though, for Logobo canoes are still on the river. They must wait and listen for hours to come. But they keep closer together now and grasp their arms sturdily, for lions have awakened and begun to yawn; there are terrible yells and shrieks, and coughing and groaning to be heard on every side, and many a plash alongside in the dark water. Sometimes a huge bat drives right against them, poisoning the air with pestiferous odour. Sometimes they see starry eyeballs glaring at them from under the plantain bushes, and hear the branches creak and crack, and the sound of stealthy footsteps near them. It is an eeriesome place this to spend even half-an-hour in after nightfall, but their only chance of safety lies in remaining perfectly still, perfectly mute. At long last light shimmers in through the leafy canopy above them, they know the moon has arisen, and it is time to be going.

Once more they are embarked, and once more stealing silently up the unknown river.

As the night advances, they are less cautious and talk more freely. Earlier in the evening they had heard the beating of the warlike tom-tom and the shouts of savage sentries, but now these are hushed and the beasts and birds of the night alone are left to rend the ear with their wild cries.

Hiding by day, and journeying silently onward and upward by night, our heroes are in less than a week far past the country of the dreaded Logobo men. Not that their dangers are over by any means, nor their trials. There are dangers from beasts, from lion or leopard, and from hideous reptiles, far more ugly than a nightmare, and these they must often face, for the rapids in the river have now become numerous, and they have to land and carry their light boat past them. But, on the whole, they were so happy now and light-hearted that they often laughed and joked and sang; and why not? Were they not marching on to fortune? They believed so, at all events.

In the long dark evenings, round the camp fire, they would lie on their blankets with their feet to the fire, and their guns not far off, you may be well sure, and sing songs and tell stories of their far-away native land. The flute, too, was put on duty, much to the delight of little Essequibo, the nigger boy. Essequibo, or Keebo as he was called for short, was at first inclined to be afraid of the flute; in fact, when first he heard it, he turned three somersaults backwards and disappeared in the jungle. He did not appear again for half-an-hour; then he came out, and gradually and slowly and wonderingly advanced to where Kenneth sat playing.

Keebo's eyes were as big as half-crown pieces, now, and he walked on tip-toe, ready to bolt again at a moment's notice.

"Massa Kennie," he said plaintively, "Massa Kennie, what you raise inside dis poor chile wid dat tube you blows into? You raisee de good spirit or de ebil one? Tell me dat."

"The good spirit, Keebo," replied Kenneth; "listen."

Then Kenneth played "The Land of the Leal."

"I'se all of a shake, Massa Kennie," said the poor boy; "de spirits, dey am all about here now, I knows. Dey not can touch poor Keebo? Tell me dat for true?"

Essequibo got more used to the flute before long, and at last he quite loved it.

Here is the story of Essequibo's conversion. I give it briefly. It was one day when Kenneth and he were alone, all the rest being away in the bush in search of food and dry fuel.

Keebo squatted near Kenneth's knees, leaning his hands thereon with child-like confidence, and gazing up into the young Scot's face as he played low sweet Scottish airs. These plaintive airs took Kenneth away back in fancy to grand Glen Alva, and the tears rose to his eyes as he thought of his childhood's days, of his simple happiness while herding sheep, of his dear mother, of Kooran and the fairy knoll.

NEW LONDON.

And last but not least of the sweet child Jessie, and of that day among the Highland heather, when she gave him the flowers. He took the Bible from his bosom and opened it.

And there they were side by side. And they were near a chapter his mother used often to read to him. His mother? Heigho! he would never see her again in this world, but faith pointed upwards.

He took his flute more cheerfully now, and began to play that sweet melody "New London." His whole soul was breathed into the instrument.

When he looked again at Keebo, why, there were tears rolling down the boy's cheeks.

"You remember *your* mother, Keebo?"

"Ess, Massa Kennie, I 'member she. De cruel Arab men kill she wid one spear. Sometimes Keebo tink she speak to her boy yet in his dreams."

"So she does, Keebo. So she does, dear child. She lives, Keebo."

"She lib, sah! My moder lib?"

TROPICAL FOLIAGE.

Then Kenneth told Essequibo the Bible tale and all the sweet story of Jesu's love; and every word sank deep into Keebo's heart, and was never, never forgotten.

When returning that day from the bush in Indian file, Archie, who was first, checked the others with uplifted hands, and pointed through the plantain bushes to the clearing where Kenneth knelt in prayer beside the boy Keebo.

Both Archie and Harvey doffed their caps, and stood reverently there, not daring to reveal their presence till Kenneth had arisen. The very sky above them seemed at that moment a holy sky.

Essequibo was a strange name to give this nigger boy. (The name of a river in South America.) It came by chance, and suited him well. He was clever, this lad; and proved a treasure to the little expedition in many a trial. His English was not of the purest, he had learnt it in Zanzibar; but he could talk the languages of the interior tribes and Arabic as well. It is truly wonderful how soon boys of this caste learn languages.

Zona was guide and chief of the party; he knew the land well, and he knew the river. He knew which way to go to avoid unfriendly Indians, and he knew also the shortest tracks. So you may fancy them going on and on day after day in their search for the land of gold, sometimes gliding along the silent and unknown river, sometimes plunging into deep, dark forests; at other times toiling over arid plains, round the spurs of lofty mountains, or wading deep through miry marsh lands, the home, *par excellence*, of the most loathsome of Saurian monsters; but journeying ever with light hearts, for hope still pointed onwards.

At night, by the camp fire, Archie and Kenneth used to build aerial castles, and plan out the kind of future that they should spend in Scotland when they had wealth. But never a night passed without a chapter being read, a psalm sung, and a prayer said. Zona used to retire to the bush, and it is but fair to say that, according to his lights, he was as good at heart as any of the others.

They had hired over a dozen sturdy Indians to carry boats and ammunition, but these men needed watching, both by night and by day. They were necessary evils, that is all. Not that negroes of this kind are not often faithful enough, but they need a master eye to guide them, else they soon lose heart and faint and fail—then fly.

More than once Keebo prevented these men from stampeding, for Keebo was ever watchful.

For many weeks our heroes kept on in the same slow course, defying every obstacle. They were now little more than fifty miles from the goal of their desires.

"If gold or diamonds," said Kenneth to Archie, "be but half as plentiful as represented, we have only to collect and retire. We have overcome every danger, and avoided the greatest danger of all—the Logobo country. We will go more swiftly down stream than we came up."

Archie was quite as hopeful as Kenneth.

Harvey hardly so much so.

"'There is many a slip 'twixt the cup and the lip,'" the latter would say.

Perhaps this was one of the happiest periods of the lives of either of our heroes. Indeed, their existence at present resembled nothing so much as one long picnic. They were like the wild creatures around them; they lived on the good things they found, and were contented and happy.

Kenneth, true lover of nature, could never have dreamt of scenery like that which he now gazed on daily. Oh the luxuriance of an African tropical woodland! what pen could describe, what pencil or brush portray it!

THE NOONTIDE SIESTA.

Yes, there were deadly things to be avoided, but one gets careless of even them, or, at least, used to them, so that in time not even a great snake dangling from a branch in front of him makes him shudder; nor is he greatly alarmed if he comes suddenly on the African "tiger," as the leopard is called, enjoying a siesta at noon-tide under a tree.

The tribes they had hitherto encountered were non-warlike and quiet. One day, however, Essequibo, who had been scouting on ahead, came rushing back in a state of great alarm.

"Dey come, dey come!" he shouted; "plenty bad men. Plenty spear and shield. Dey kill and eat us all for true!"

The carrier negroes threw down their boat and packages and would have bolted *en masse*, had not our heroes stood by them with pistol and whip. The whip was, I believe, more dreaded than even the revolver.

In less time than it takes me to tell it, the little expedition, which was quickly formed into a solid square, was surrounded by a cloud of armed blacks.

To fight such a mob was out of the question; they used better tactics: they pretended to be overjoyed at meeting them. They were friends, Kenneth told the chief of these negroes, not foes, and wanted to see the king, and brought him presents from the far-off white man's land.

Shouts of joy from those simple natives now rent the air, and rattling their spears against their shields they led the way towards the camp of the king, a village of adobe and grass huts, built round cocoa-nut palms, in the midst of a great and fertile plain. In the centre of the town, inside a compound, was the square bungalow of King 'Ntango.

'Ntango was in, but did not appear for hours. It would not be royal etiquette to show much curiosity. Meanwhile the native women brought milk and honey and baked plantains, and everything went as merry as a marriage bell.

The king, into whose presence they were ushered at last, was round and squat, very yellow and very fat.

He showered his questions on Kenneth through Essequibo as interpreter.

Where did they come from? What did they want? Were they Arab or foreign? Did they come to steal his wives and little ones? How long did they want to stop? For ever, of course. Where were the gifts? Guns? Yes. Beads? Good. Pistols? Good again. But was this all? Where was the rum? Arab men had been here before, they brought much good rum. What, *no* rum? Never a skin of *rum*? Ugh!

With this last ejaculation, which was almost a shriek, the king sprang from the mat on which he had squatted.

"They must die?" he shouted; "die every one of them. The Arab must first die, then the black men. Then the white men. Essequibo he would fatten and kill and eat. Bring chains; away with them! *away*! away! AWAY!"

The king's eyes shot fire as he waved his arms aloft, and shouted, "*Away*, away!" and his lips were flecked with blood and foam.

He was a fearful being to behold, this irate African savage.

Almost at the same moment our heroes were seized rudely from behind, disarmed, and dragged off. They soon found themselves huddled together in one room, with stone walls, slimy, damp, and over-run with creeping things that made them shudder, albeit they were under the very shadow of death.

Towards evening the king sent to "comfort" them; it was very condescending of him. The "comfort" lay in the information that at sunrise next day they would be led out to die, by spear or by knife, as they might choose.

Meanwhile, poor Essequibo's chains were knocked off, and he was led away to his fattening pen.

Such is life in Central Africa. But stranger things still befell our heroes.

Chapter Twenty
Land of Darkness

Scene: The interior of King 'Ntango's palace. The king seated on a mat in the middle of the floor of the principal apartment—a large square room with walls of mud and grass. The only furniture, a tall tom-tom, a mat-covered dais, and a heap of empty stone bottles in a corner. Those bottles once contained gin.

It is near sunset, the king is alone. There is no sound to break the silence, except the tap, tap, tap the gecko lizards that crawl on the walls make, as they beat to death the moths they catch.

Yes, the king is alone in his glory, though his spear-armed attendants wait outside. He is quite a study, this savage potentate, to any one fond of an anthropology. Look at him now! he is leaning his fat face on his podgy fingers, his elbows are resting on his knees—he is thinking.

There are but two things in this world that this king dearly loves; one is to see human blood spilled, the other is to drink gin or rum. These last two words are the only English ones he can pronounce or understand. He learnt them from itinerant Arabs, unscrupulous scoundrels, who bought the youth and flower of his people for a bottle each.

The king is thinking; the question that exercises his mind at present is this, "Shall I kill these white men, and laugh to see the red blood flow; or keep two, and send the others back for rum?"

"Room," this is how he pronounces the word "rum," and "gin" he calls "geen."

"Room, room, room," he mutters to himself, "geen, geen, geen."

He rises; a thought strikes him. May it not be possible that one, just one full bottle remains still among that heap of empty ones? He goes straight to the heap, and turns them over. No, not one. Still, he has a glimmering notion that in a dazed moment he hid one. Ha! he remembers all of a sudden. He seizes the stick with which he is wont to beat the tom-tom, and hies him to a corner, and speedily unearths, not one bottle, but two.

He is a joyful king now. He whacks the tom-tom, and summons two of his wives to squat beside him; not to help him to drink, but to *see* him drink.

Then he summons Essequibo, and launches questions at him. "How long will he take to fatten? How long before he be ready to kill? Do the white men tremble to die?"

"No," Keebo tells him; "they rejoice to die because their spirits will go to a glorious land of flowers and sunshine."

The king gets blue with rage. He whacks Keebo with the tom-tom stick, and he whacks his wives; then he declares that the white men shall *not* die, that their spirits shall *not* go to the glorious land of flowers and sunshine.

Then he drinks "geen," and cools down.

But Keebo sees his advantage. He expatiates on the mechanical ability and cleverness of white men in general, and of Massa Kennie, Archie, and Harvey in particular, and so inflames the king's cupidity, that he sends for the white men, and has their chains knocked off in his presence, and tells his sentries they are free, and any one who touches the hem of their garments shall be made food for the blue-bottle flies, and the long-legged "krachaw." (A kind of carrion-eating heron.)

"Ha! ha! ha!" he yells, "the king will live for ever."

Then he drinks again, yells again, whacks his wives with the tom-tom stick, and laughs to see them wince; and drinks, and drinks, and drinks, till he falls back asleep, and is borne away by the wives he whacked, and laid tenderly on the daïs.

"Well," cried Harvey, "this is a queer ending to a day's march."

Zona shrugs his square thin shoulders, and Kenneth and Archie laugh.

"Ask those scoundrels," says Kenneth to Essequibo, "what they have done with our arms and our boat."

Very submissive are those spear-armed warriors now. They lead them to a wood, and there in the thicket they find everything intact.

"Now, lads, do as I tell you," said Kenneth.

And here is what our heroes did at Kenneth's advice. They rolled all their spare arms and ammunition in blankets, dug a hole, buried them, and turned the boat upside down on them. Next they tore up a lot of white and red rags, tied them to strings, and arranged these along, over, and around the boat, in precisely the way you would over a row of peas in the country to keep the sparrows away.

Funny though it may seem, this was quite enough to keep these savage negroes at bay. There was magic in it, they thought, and they gave that wood a wide berth.

Well, our heroes had, after a manner of speaking, to buy their lives.

The king had them before him at daybreak, not to order them to execution, but to give them his royal commands. They were to teach his people to do all the clever things that white men could do; if they failed, the king told them death would be the fate of their teachers.

"We do not fear to die, King 'Ntango," said Kenneth.

The king looked at him with a merry twinkle in his eye; then he took a sip of "geen" and said, through the interpreter Keebo, —

"You do not fear death? No, you think you go straight to your glorious land of sunshine; but listen, you will *not*. I will arrange it differently. I will cut from you a leg, an arm, and an ear, — ha! ha! what think you? will the leg, and arm, and ear go first to the land of sunshine, and wait you? Take care, I am a great king, and I have twenty thousand ways to torture without killing."

Poor Kenneth confessed to himself that the king had the best of the argument, but he replied, —

"If you cut from me an arm or leg, how then shall I teach your people?"

The king smiled grimly, and said, "Go."

They must propitiate this king, that was evident, in order to gain his favour and their eventual liberty, for slaves they now undoubtedly were to all intents and purposes.

So they set themselves to teach his people to build boats, and sail on the great lake that occupied the centre of the plain; to make articles of furniture and household utility generally; to till the ground and to sow; and lastly, to cook the latter department belonged to Zona, and it greatly pleased the king. It pleased him also to see his men drilled, and to witness their deftness in rowing and sailing, but he saw not the sense of sowing.

SHOOTING THE LEOPARD.

"Has not the Great Spirit," he said to Kenneth, "given us the fruits that grow aloft on the trees, the fish in the water, and the beasts of the field? what need we of more?"

But days rolled into weeks, and weeks into months. The prospect of getting out of this king's country, either onward to the gold country, or back towards the coast, seemed to get less and less bright. 'Ntango's men became good soldiers, adept spearsmen; formerly they could send an arrow with terrible precision through a kind of blow-pipe into the breast of a leopard or lion; now they were not afraid to attack these creatures with the spear alone.

But these better soldiers of the king's were all the better able to watch their prisoners; there was no end to the king's cunning. Many and many a plan did Kenneth and his brothers in affliction fall upon to try to effect their escape, but every one was frustrated.

"No," said the king to Kenneth, — "I love you so much now I cannot part with you. You must live with me for ever and ever and ever."

This was, indeed, a dark prospect.

A whole year passed away; *the* one comfort of their lives now rested in the fact that they were permitted to enjoy each other's company. They had built quite a splendid bungalow for themselves, and surrounded it with a beautiful compound and gardens, in which the most delightful flowers bloomed, and where grew the most delicious fruit. Under other circumstances their lives would really have been enjoyable. Wild sports they had also in abundance, and fishing and boating both by lake and on the river, but on these excursions one hundred of the king's trustiest spearmen always accompanied them, and their bungalow was surrounded by a palisade that *they* did not build, and for ever guarded by sentries they could not elude.

One good for these poor people Kenneth did effect; he had a meeting-house built, and therein, Sabbath after Sabbath, he taught them to read and to pray, just as he had taught good Essequibo.

It was not long before the king found out Kenneth's powers as a musician, and at first it was hard on Kenneth, for he was kept playing from morning till night for weeks.

Music lost its power to some extent over the king at length, and latterly it was but rarely he sent for his musician to play. Nor had 'Ntango much of an ear for melody, for Kenneth manufactured a score of "chanters" out of pieces of cane, and taught a score of savages to make an unearthly kind of noise in all kinds of keys; and this pleased the king quite as much as the flute.

Archie thought of a plan at last to get a brief holiday. The first intimation of it was given the king by Essequibo. All the white men, he told him one morning, were ill and dying, and nothing would cure them but permission to explore the country to the nor'-west, the land where gold lay.

The king graciously gave his permission, and the expedition, well guarded, started to prospect for gold. After days and days of toil and travel they reached the El Dorado.

Disappointment and nothing else. Gold there was, but not for the gathering; it was deeply imbedded in veins of quartz, and the strongest machinery would be needed to work it.

Diamonds there were none.

Their gloom increased now. Their hopes of finding fortune had been but a youthful dream, and had ended in making them prisoners to a wild and despotic savage.

If there was any one ray now to illuminate their darkness and despair, it lay in the fact that their visit to the land of darkness had not been quite in vain; they had sowed the seeds of righteousness, and who could say what fruit these might not bear in after-times?

They tried now to make the best of their position, and take things as they came, determined, however, if a chance should arise, to seek safety in flight at all hazards. The river was not far away, and their boat and spare ammunition still lay intact and handy.

Nearly two years passed away.

One night they had retired to their bungalow early. It was Archie's birthday, and they were going to have a big talk about home.

It was long past twelve o'clock before they thought of lying down. Ere they undressed they went for a walk as usual in their garden, to breathe the odour of the flowers, which the dews of evening never failed to draw out.

The moon was high in the heavens, looking like a little burnished shield in the blue sky, and dimming the light of the thousand twinkling stars. Suddenly from every direction there arose a muttering startled cry, which presently increased to a yell. Smoke, too, began to roll across the sky, increasing every moment, while tongues of flame leaped higher and higher.

They listened thunderstruck.

"Logobo—Logobo—Logobo!" That was the terrible cry.

"Heaven be praised!" cried Kenneth. "Now, boys, now, *men*, our time has come for freedom or for death. Follow me!"

He grasped his rifle as he spoke, and rushed out. The sentries had fled.

The whole village was in flames, and in the lurid glare, hand to hand in deathly combat, struggled two tribes of savages.

It was no business of our heroes, however. They rushed onwards through the *melée*, and in a very short time had reached and shouldered their boat.

One hour after, the din of the conflict was muffled in the distance, miles away, and Kenneth and his companions were safe on the river.

They were not free yet, however. Swiftly down the river they sped, racing onwards at all hazards. Daylight found them far away, but not safe. All the country they passed through gave token of the march into the interior of the Logobo men. The villages by the banks were fire-blackened ruins, swollen corpses floated here and there, and half-charred spars.

A week of fearful toil and anxiety, during which they had more adventures and hair-breadth escapes than I could describe in a goodly volume, brought them to the edge of the Logobo land. And here redoubled caution was needed. They could not rush it, as they had done the other part of the river. They must resort to their old tactics of hiding by day and pursuing their way adown the unknown river in the silence of night.

But three days of this work had almost set them free. It was the very last day of their hiding, and near sunset. They had determined to start early, and were longing for six o'clock and speedy darkness. Lower and lower went the sun. Already the gloom of the short twilight was settling down on the still forest, and beasts of prey were beginning to wake up, and yawn—and a fearful sound it is to listen to—when suddenly into the clearing where they stood strutted a Logobo savage in war array.

The yell he gave awakened a thousand others on every side. The whole forest was alive with savages apparently.

"Ping, ping," from Archie's revolver, and down dropped the Logobo warrior.

"Quick, men, quick," cried Kenneth, "to boat, to boat!"

Ah! none too soon; hardly had they launched their frail craft and embarked, ere a flight of spears came from the bush, and poor Essequibo fell.

The gathering darkness favoured them, and they were soon beyond the reach of danger.

Two hours after, the moon had risen; its rays brightened the woods and rocks and sparkled on the river.

Poor Keebo lay in the bottom of the boat across Zona's knee, his face upturned to the sky.

His life was ebbing fast away.

Near him knelt Kenneth, holding his cold hand.

"I'se goin', good-bye," murmured the dying lad. "I'se goin' to de land—ob sunshine. I see poor mudder soon."

"Keebo," said Kenneth, "you know me?"

"Ess, dear Massa Kennie."

"Now, say after me. O Lord!"

"'O Lor'!'"

"Receive poor Keebo's soul."

"'Poor Keebo's soul.'"

"For the blessed Jesu's sake."

"'De bressed Jesu's sake.'"

There was just one little painful quiver of the limbs, then a gentle soughing sigh, and—Keebo was gone.

Chapter Twenty One
Camp-Life in the Far West

Scene: In the backwoods of British America. Kenneth, Archie, and Harvey are seen sitting around the camp fire. It is a whole hour after sunset, and yet there is plenty of light in the sky. There are rocks and pine trees around, a brawling stream not far off. There is a tall rugged mountain in the distance; its highest peaks are snow-clad. Southwards away, grey clouds are heaped up on the horizon, a slight scimitar-shaped moon is shining in the north-west, and ominous little dark clouds are drifting over it. It is not from this moon that the light comes, but from a strange yellowish after-glow, which tinges all the western horizon, and, mingling with the blue above, evolves a peculiar shade of green.

"Heap more wood on the fire, Archie," said Kenneth. "I'm growing quite an old man, I think. It is only a year since we left Africa and rounded the Horn, hardly nine months since we bade adieu to civilisation, and became wanderers and vagabonds in this wild dreary land, gold-hunting as usual, and yet it seems to me an age."

Kenneth pulled his blanket closer round his shoulders as he spoke, and Archie rose to replenish the fire, laughing as he did so.

"When *you* die of old age," he said, "I shall make my will, Kennie boy."

"Oh! but we are sure to find gold," put in Harvey.

"Well, I don't know, but it seems to me that this searching for gold is like chasing a wild goose or a will-o'-the-wisp. Don't you think, Archie, we had better settle down to something more certain if more slow?"

"*I do* think so," replied Archie; "and after what Harvey here has told us, that he is the son of poor old Laird McGregor, and rightful heir to the McGregor estates, *he* ought to go straight away home, turn that old Yankee tyrant out, and regain possession of his own. You cannot break an entail, you know."

"Heigho!" sighed Harvey, "I have repented my quarrel with my dear old father all my life. It was my proud Highland blood that caused it in the first instance. I rushed away to sea, I changed my name, I made myself out as dead. I thought not of the kind heart I was breaking, of the grey hairs I was bringing down in sorrow to the grave. And how has fate rewarded me? I have been a rover ever since, a wanderer and a vagabond; thrice have riches been within my grasp, thrice has Fortune dashed the cup aside. And am I to go now that my father is in his long home and claim my patrimony? My pride forbids; I'd rather be a ghillie on the old estate, or a keeper, than proud laird of it all."

"Stay," said Kenneth, laying his hand kindly on Harvey's shoulder. "Not for your own sake should you do this thing, but remember you have a mother and sister, still alive it is to be hoped. Do you never think of them?"

Harvey's hands now covered his face, his form was bent forward, but the heaving of his chest told of the grief that was rending him.

"Think, too, of the Clachan restored, of the old church bell once more calling the people of the glen to worship on the Sabbath mornings. Steve the Yankee, from all accounts, is a tyrant, an oppressor, and a villain. Harvey McGregor, think of seeing your old mother once more in the dear old-fashioned pew."

"Kenneth McAlpine!" cried Harvey, starting up, "no more of this now, you irritate, you madden me!

"But," he added, in a more softened tone of voice, "I may promise you just one thing. If we fail this time, if *I* fail to find fortune, I will return to my mother like the prodigal son I have been. Though fain, oh! how fain I would be to return full-handed, *rich*!"

"Thank you, Harvey, thank you for this promise. And now for your sake and for all our sakes I trust that fortune will at length favour us."

The conversation then wandered back to the old, old theme; home at Glen Alva. A strange life these three adventurers had led for the last nine months and over. Wandering from place to place, sleeping by night in the open air when the weather was fine, in caves or huts of pine-wood branches when wet, and sojourning with trappers or even in the wigwams of the Indian when snow covered the ground and the storm winds were howling.

Wandering from place to place prospecting, wandering on and on in search of gold. A strange wild life was theirs, but it suited their tastes; then there was an ever-present hope that had not yet deserted them, a hope and an ambition to become suddenly wealthy as many a man had done before them. Yes, it is true, many a one had found gold and silver, but tens of thousands had found an early grave in searching for it.

Harvey, or let us call him now Harvey McGregor, was in a manner of speaking a genius. He possessed originality of thought, and he never hesitated to put his ideas to the test. He felt sure of one thing, namely, that gold and silver mines were not entirely confined to the southern states of North America. He had found treasure among the mountains of British Columbia, and he meant, so he said, to find it again in such quantities that both he and his friends would be "millionaires in a month." But luck seemed long of coming. They had wandered all the way from California, and encountered every imaginable danger, in moor and mountain, forest, flood, and fall; and here they were to-night, with no other worldly wealth than the blankets they would presently roll themselves up in, and their guns with a modicum of ammunition.

IN THE FAR WEST.

Only they had youth and health on their side, though even these seemed passing away from poor McGregor. Grief had done its turn; it had hollowed his cheek, and though barely twenty-five, silver threads were already appearing in his brown beard.

"Now pile more wood on the fire, Archie dear lad, and we will go to sleep like good boys, and dream we are back in our dear old glen."

Archie did as told, and before long all three were sound asleep. They did not care even to do sentry duty. They trusted all to fate.

Silence now, except for the wind soughing through the tall mysterious-looking pine trees, or the occasional bark of fox or scream of night bird. A great cinnamon bear about midnight came snuffing around; he could have rent our sleeping heroes in pieces, but there was nothing cooking to lure him towards the fire. A stray wolf came next, and actually leapt over Kenneth's legs. He was picking up some scraps of food when McGregor moaned and tossed, and away went the wolf.

"I had such a dream," cried McGregor next morning. "I say, boys, I told you there was a bank of gold up here, and I for one start digging to-day."

So he did, and so did all.

The only possible place to commence operations lay close to the banks of a turbulent river that came winding down through a pine-clad mountain land.

Silently, almost solemnly the trio worked, speaking but little, hanging on to their pipes (if I may use so strange a phrase), and hanging on to spade, and pick, and shovel.

THE LOG-HUT HOME.

All that day, and next, and next. About the coming of the fourth day, there was a shout from McGregor's claim.

"Hurrah, boys! Hurrah, boys! Run here, lads, run here!"

They did run.

McGregor held up before their astonished gaze a nugget of almost pure gold as big as a baby's shoe.

More gold was found every day for a week, and in gradually increasing quantities. They were already in possession of about three hundred pounds' worth. No wonder they rejoiced. No wonder they were merry.

Now, around the camp fire, what stories are told, what songs are sung, what castles in the air are built!

They will all be millionaires. Archie says he is going to have a nice mansion down in the Clachan, and close by the riverside, and will fish there and in the sea just as when he was a boy. Nothing will satisfy Kenneth but a house near the fairy knoll. He pulls out the old Bible, Nannie's gift, and opens it. There lie the withered flowers, and looking at them sets him a-thinking and a-wondering and a-dreaming.

"Little Jessie," he says to himself, "can she still be alive? Is it possible she might one day be mine?"

He restores the flowers, restores the Book of books, and lies back to gaze at the starry sky and think.

But he is not allowed to.

"Out with the flute, Kennie," cries Archie. "Oh, play me some dear auld Scottish lilt, that will make tears of joy well up in our eyes?"

Kenneth plays tune after tune, air after air; and then the trio join voices and sing "My native Highland home" till the woods ring and pine trees nod, and distant rocks send back the chorus.

There is hardly any need of a blanket to-night, for the day has been hot, and look, even now clouds are rolling slowly up and hiding the half-moon. Great round clouds they are, and little dark water-dog clouds lie nearer the earth, and seem to perch and leap from top to top of the pine trees, like birds of evil omen.

THE SPATE.

A storm is brewing.

By-and-bye, from far over the hills comes the muttering growl of distant thunder. Presently clouds go scurrying overhead, and a bright flash is followed by a rattling peal.

Rain, and terrible rain, followed, and the wind began to rise. The camp fire is drowned out, and our trio are fain to seek the shelter of a cave on the wooded hillside. None too soon; with a crashing roar, louder and more continued than any thunder ever heard, the storm bursts upon them with hurricane force. And all that night it continues. The pine trees have fallen in all directions. The river has risen in spate. Through the darkness they can see the ghostly glimmer of its foam, and they can hear the hurtling sound of the mighty boulders as they roll along.

Morning came at last, grim and grey.

"Saint Mary! what a scene is here!"

The whole face of the country is altered in appearance. Where is their claim, their gold mine, their hope of fortune, their joy of the previous evening? All swept away or buried in chaos.

Just three weeks after this fearful storm Kenneth and Archie bade good-bye to their friend and comrade Harvey McGregor. He had given up all hopes of finding fortune, and was returning to Scotland to claim his property.

They bade him good-bye at New Westminster. Then, hand in hand as if they were boys once more, they turned their backs to the coast, and went away towards the mountains.

"Archie," said Kenneth, "there is gold to be got among these hills, but *not* by digging."

"You are right."

"Let us work for our fortune like steady, brave men. It may come, or it may not. At all events, we will be better working. And we will try to forget the past and build no more castles in the air."

"Agreed," said Archie; "let us work."

At Victoria these two brave young men changed the few nuggets they had found for coin. Then they pushed their way many miles inland in Columbia, and, having hired servants and bought a little land with plenty more to purchase lying right behind it, they set to work with a will. They built their house, a solid log-mansion. They planned and laid out their gardens. They hewed timber, and sawed it, and sent it down stream. They tore the roots from the ground and cleared it for grain, and, in a word, settled down in every way as farmers, determined to make the best of every chance.

And here, in their far-away western home, let us leave them for a while, and journey over the broad Atlantic with Harvey McGregor. There are those in Scotland whose lives and actions may not be quite devoid of interest to many who have read this history from the commencement.

Chapter Twenty Two
Glen Alva under New Government

"The tables were drawn, it was idlesse all,
Knight and page and household squire
Loitered through the lofty hall,
Or crowded round the ample fire.
The stag-hounds, weary of the chase,
Lay stretched upon the rushy floor,
And urged in dreams the forest race,
From Teviot Stone to Eskdale moor."

Walter Scott.

Scene: The tartan parlour of an old Highland mansion in the west of Scotland. Wine and walnuts on the table. About a dozen gentlemen seated round in attitudes of ease and enjoyment. A great fire of coal and oak logs in the low and spacious grate. From their accent these gentlemen are mostly English and American.

"Robinson!" cried Mr Steve, who was seated at the head of the table, and whose sparkling eyes and flushed cheeks told a tale that was far from difficult to read, "Robinson, the bottle is with you. What think you of the stuff? I paid thirty dollars a dozen for it at old Clintock's sale, and I guess you'll hardly match it in this country, if anywheres. Donald," he continued, addressing a white-haired old Highland servant, who stood near, "heap more wood on the fire, and look active. Don't stand and stare like the log figure on a tobacconist's sign. Move your joints, I say."

Donald hastened to do as he was told; but as he obeyed he muttered something in the Gaelic language, of which the following is a pretty fair translation.

"It is Donald's own self that would like to put *you* on the fire. Truth told, and it is then."

"Yes," replied Robinson, a wealthy draper from London, "the wine is truly excellent, and if I were to speak the truth now, I'd say earnestly that I don't think we *could* match it in our old country."

"And after all, you know," said a white-faced, meek young man, who sat near Mr Steve, "this country is vewy nearly worn out."

"Oh! for the matter of that now," said Steve, "America, above all countries for institooshuns, great armies, great navies—if we chose to build them—for tall mountains, broad lakes, big steamboats, and mighty rivers."

"Heah! heah!" from several voices.

"England," continued Steve, "is all very well to spend money in, 'cause you're near the Continent, and can run 'most anywhere without the trouble of crossing much water. But I say America's the country to make the money in."

"Heah! heah!"

"And, after all, what, I ask, would England be without America?"

"What, indeed?"

"Yet, *I* wouldn't boast. Your true American never does. You Englishmen, pardon me, talk about the sun never setting on British territory, of your drum rolling and your reveillé beating in a cordon right round the globe, and of your owning the sixth part of the land of this boundless universe, and *all* the water. Now, if that ain't boasting—and mebbe it ain't—it is what I'd call pretty tall talk."

STEVE'S DEERHOUND.

The laugh became general at this speech of Mr Steve of Glen Alva, and every face beamed.

"You must all come out next spring, gentlemen, and stay a few weeks in my New York mansion. Nay, I won't take a refusal from one of you. So there! And I guess, too, I can give you a good time of it."

A beautiful deerhound rose slowly up from the mat and leaned his great head on the table. He did not wish to join the conversation. He was only craving a biscuit.

Steve flicked a walnut at the head, which struck the poor animal on the eye, and evidently caused him great pain. He did not howl, however—Scotch deerhounds are far too game for that; but he shut his eye, which watered a deal, and went and lay down again on the rug with a big sigh, and all the rest of the evening was engaged licking his pastern, and applying it tenderly to the eye. This is a dog's way of administering a warm fomentation.

"Capital shot, eh?" laughed Steve.

"Yes," from some of his guests.

"But I say, you know, Mr Steve," said one, with probably something of kindness to God's lower creation in his heart, "I say, it wouldn't do to go to the hill with blind dogs. Would it?"

"Oh! he won't hurt. It takes a deal to hurt these hounds. They are like the Scots themselves, very hardy and active, but precious lazy. Just look at all those dogs snoring round the fire.

"I've cleared the glen, though, of some of the lazy Scots. Why, it is doing them good to drum them off to America. In my opinion, more'n one half of Scotland should be cleared and planted out in forest."

"Well," said one Englishman, "maybe you're right; and now, as myself and most of us are going south early to-morrow morning, might I suggest that we join the ladies? But before I go, I must just take the liberty of thanking Mr Steve, our kindly-hearted host, for his hospitality to us since we've been down here, and roamed in, and shot over, his magnificent forest. I consider Mr Steve's hospitality to be far more than princely, both out-doors and in. Just think, gentlemen, we have had to our guns about one hundred and thirty-six stags, and as we all know every stag costs its owner 300 pounds (so it is said in Scotland) you can compute what Mr Steve's hospitality costs him. I say no more."

"A mere flea-bite," returned Mr Steve pompously; "I'll have you all again next year; and now supposing we *do* join the ladies."

Mr Steve's household was certainly kept up in a right lordly style. There was no stint in it of anything that was good. He had any number of beef-eating servants. He was a good customer to his tradesmen—including his wine merchant,—who all, however, lived in Glasgow or London. It must, therefore, be confessed that he brought money into the country, and in this way did good; yet he was not liked in the glens nor villages, nor much relished by the proud old Highland families. He was no friend to the poor man, and his minions had been known ere now to shoot stray pet dogs, and even cudgel to death the cats of poor old lone women,—cats that probably were the only friends and companions they had in this world. So, to put it plain, Mr Steve was *not* liked in the neighbourhood, and reference was often made of, and fond memories went back to, the dear old days, when good Laird McGregor owned the glen—now a wilderness,—when it was dotted over with peaceful if rustic cottages, from which, as sure as sunrise, every morning rose, with the smoke from the chimneys the song of praise to Him Who loves the poor man as well as the rich.

AUTUMN IN A SCOTCH FOREST.

The guests were preparing to retire, when a liveried servant entered with a card on a gold salver.

"Beg pardon, sir, but the gentleman would insist upon my presenting that 'ere card."

"Take it away," said Mr Steve, reading the card, without even deigning to finger it. "Take it away. I can see no one to-night."

"I'll tell him, sir; but on'y, sir, he said his business was of immense importance to yourself, and that he were a-going south by first train to-morrow morning."

"Heigho!" sighed Steve, moving towards the door. "What a bore! You'll excuse me half a moment, gentlemen?"

The stranger had been shown into the low-ceilinged but snug old-fashioned parlour, and rose and bowed as Steve entered.

"I presume," he said, "I have the honour of addressing Mr Steve?"

"You have," said Mr Steve; "and pray be brief, for my guests wait."

"My business is of a private nature," replied the stranger, with a glance at the servant.

At a nod from his master the latter retired.

The stranger took the liberty of shutting the door, then confronted Mr Steve.

He was a youngish man, of bold and gentlemanly appearance, and unmistakably Scotch, though with slightly foreign action while conversing.

SCENE IN GLEN ALVA.

"Mr Steve," he said, "I will be very brief. I might have communicated with you through my solicitor, but thought it more fair to you, and more honourable in me, to come personally, for, after all, when you hear what I have to say, litigation will be unnecessary."

"Litigation, sir? Pray go on," said Steve, smiling somewhat sarcastically. "You're not out of your mind, are you?"

"You shall judge for yourself. You purchased this estate of Alva, sir, from the late Laird McGregor?"

"I did, and paid for it handsomely."

"But by the laws of this country entailed estates cannot be sold and the entail thus broken, unless it can be proved that no other male heir lives. Thus in point of fact, at all events, were the lands and estates of Alva left by will to the McGregors and their lineal descendants."

"See, stranger," said Steve, "I'm not going to debate here all night on matters of law. Law is a dry subject at best. I bought Alva, there was *no* other male heir to McGregor, and his only son was drowned at sea."

"His only son now stands before you!"

"Then the father—"

"Stay," cried young McGregor, "tempt me not to do that I should be sorry for. I came but to inform you I would make every attempt to win back my own. I have now to say good-night."

"I thank you," sneered Steve, "for your courtesy; but do—*not*—fear—you. Good-night."

Chapter Twenty Three
The Wanderer's Return

"Dear land of my birth, far from thee have I been,
By streamlets so flowery and valleys so green,
In vain seeking fortune; but still as of yore
The home of my heart is the Vale of Strathmore."

Old Scottish Song.

Scene: Sunset on the sea. So close to the ocean is the old castle built that, looking from the window which almost overhangs it, nothing else can be seen but the golden-tipped waves, golden-tipped even to the far-off horizon, and breaking with pleasing murmur on the beach beneath. The mountains that rise inland from the castle are either wholly green, or patched with purple heather. In a room overlooking the sea, in high-backed cushioned chair, sits a lady,—but little past the prime of life, perhaps, though her hair is like the snow. Her face is very pleasant to behold, so calm and resigned is it. Near her on a stool a maid is reading to her.

"I think now, Mary," said the lady at last, "it is time to order tea."

Mary, a modest, wee Highland maiden, rose, and quietly retired.

As she opened the door a great black-as-jet Newfoundland came bounding in, all white teeth and eager eyes. He went straight away, and placed his head on his mistress's lap, and was gently caressed.

"Where have you been, Bran?" she said. "Not in the sea at this time of night? But you do go in sometimes later, you know, and then hie away to the kitchen, sly dog, to get your coat dried before you come to see me."

Mary tapped at the door and entered. Her face was bright with pleasure.

"Oh! Mrs McGregor," she said, "Mr Smith has come by steamer from Oban!"

Mrs McGregor's face assumed an expression of great seriousness.

"Oh!" she cried, "I trust it is no bad news he brings about my brother."

"No, no," the girl hastened to say; "he bade me tell you it was all a visit of pleasure. I showed him to the old room, and he will be here in a few minutes."

Mr Smith, I may tell the reader, was family solicitor to Mrs McGregor's brother, in whose house she had resided since her husband's death. The solicitor lived in London, but not unfrequently ran down to enjoy the sea or the land sport, so easily obtained in this lone but lovely isle of the Hebrides.

"Surprised to see me, Mrs McGregor?" said the gentleman, as he shook hands and sat down. "Hope I didn't frighten you much? Just ran down from town to get a mouthful of sea-air. Been rather overworked of late. Tea, did you say? Yes, with pleasure, but Mary must really bring me something substantial to go along with it. My journey has made me hungry."

"And you have seen my brother?"

"Only two days ago, and he is looking hale and hearty, and hopes to return in a week."

"Well, Mr Smith, you must stay here till he returns."

"It is doubtful if I can; business, you know, business. What a lovely sunset, to be sure! Bodes a fine day to-morrow I should think."

"You seem happy, Mr Smith?"

"I feel as fresh as a daisy."

"And yet, but a minute ago, you hinted at being fagged by over-work."

"Oh!" replied the solicitor, shaking his head, "that was *before* I left town. Bless you, madam, two gulps of Highland air set me on my legs again at any time."

The two chatted very pleasantly together over the evening meal; but towards the end of it Mr Smith managed adroitly to turn the conversation to bygone times.

"I seem to sadden you though," he said.

"Oh! no: I'm resigned to everything now. My time will not be very long, and I know the good God in whom I trust has done all for the best. But the loss of my son was a great blow; then my husband's death."

"Why, Mrs McGregor, do you make that distinction? You talk of your husband's death, but always speak of poor Harvey's *loss*."

"Because, Mr Smith, I saw my husband die; my son went away, and ah! foolish though it may be, I cherish half a hope he may yet return to close his mother's eyes."

"Well, well, I daresay stranger things may have happened," said the solicitor, thoughtfully looking and pretending to read a fortune in the grounds of his tea-cup.

Now, the fact is, that no sooner had Harvey McGregor left Mr Steve's than he had hurried up to town, and called on Mr Smith, the only man-at-law he knew. He speedily convinced that gentleman of his identity, and got his mother's address. Heedless Harvey would have hurried away home—as he called it—at once, but wise Mr Smith would not hear of it.

"Come a day after me," he had advised. "I'll go down and break the news, for, don't you know, my boy, that joy can kill?"

Hence Mr Smith's present visit to the old castle.

"Whose fortune are you trying to read in that tea-cup?" said Mrs McGregor, with a strange ring in her voice, a strange sparkle in her eye. "Give me the cup," she added.

She turned it round and round.

"I see," she said; "my boy's barques sailing everywhere over the world. Sometimes they are wrecked, but *he* is never drowned. I see the prows of these ships pointing everywhere, but never homeward. My boy is proud. Ah I at last here comes one, and my boy, my boy is in it!"

She almost dashed down the cup as she spoke, and sprang to her feet. "Smith," she cried, "you cannot deceive me; there is something in my breast, born of a mother's love, that tells me Harvey has come."

Mr Smith hummed and haa'ed, as the saying is, and muttered something about a letter.

"No, no, no," she cried; "you only thought you ought to break the news gently to me, but I saw strange joy in your eye as soon as you entered. Now, dear Mr Smith, I appreciate all your kindness, but you see I can bear joy as well as grief. Tell me all about it."

And the solicitor did so. At the conclusion she took out her handkerchief, and sobbed just a little.

Then she abruptly rose and left the room.

Mr Smith said never a word. He knew she had gone to pray.

Next evening they were seated together—mother and son—mother and "prodigal son," as Harvey would persist in calling himself.

Mr Smith respected their feelings. He went away to fish, and did not return till dinner-time.

But that evening the trio had much to talk about, many business matters to discuss.

"Alva shall return to its rightful owner," exclaimed Mr Smith. "I'm determined on that, if Steve were nineteen times an American millionaire. It was sold for half, nay, but fourth its value. It was sold to pay London debts of honour forsooth. Turf and otherwise. Bah! The money shall be raised to repay Mr Steve, and out he shall go, as sure as I belong to the great family of Smith. I'll employ London counsel that will astonish him. You'll see I'll do it. *Can* and *shall*. And I won't let the grass grow under my feet either."

Nor did the worthy solicitor.

He started for London the very next day, leaving Harvey and his mother alone.

Harvey felt, and almost looked, a boy again. He had so much to speak about, so much to tell of his hard adventurous life in search of fortune; and it is so pleasant to be listened to by one who loves you! No wonder Harvey McGregor felt happy. All the past blotted out and forgiven, all the future as hopeful as the past had been dark and oftentimes dismal.

With many, if not most, of his adventures, the reader is already familiar, but of his voyage home from New York I have said nothing.

Harvey then was possessed of some little money, and this he determined to convey home on his person. He might have had bills of exchange, but he was but little conversant with such aids to the transaction of business. Would he take it in gold and wear it in a waist-belt round his body? He was too old a sailor to do any such thing. For in event of being cast into the water he knew well that nothing sinks a man sooner than gold. It is the greed of gold, by the way, that sinks men on shore.

But Harvey knew the sight and feel of a crisp Bank of England note. He got these and sewed them into a waterproof bag, and this he put into a waist-belt, which he wore by night and by day.

He worked his passage home. He was no idler, and preferred work to play.

The vessel was a sailing ship, not a steamer, and bound for Glasgow. With fair winds she would fly across the wide Atlantic. And oh! how wide the Atlantic does seem to those who are homeward bound, I for one can tell from experience!

The winds *were* fair for a time; then they became baffling.

Often the *Marianne*, as she was called, had to lie to for days in a gale of wind; then fair weather would come again and all would be life and joy, fore and aft. Then round the wind would chop once more, and the sea wax fretful, angry, vicious, hitting the poor ship such vengeful blows, that she bent her head, and reeled and creaked in every timber.

Well, such is a seaman's life in a sailing ship at almost any time, and Harvey would not have minded it a bit, only he was going home, and every day was precious.

Near the coast at long last. They would (d.v.) round the Mull of Cantyre in another day, then hurrah! and hurrah! for the beautiful Clyde.

But all at once the weather waxed dark and stormy, and the wind headed round. The glass came tumbling down, and at sunset things looked black and serious.

How the waves did dash and beat to be sure, and how the wind did rave and roar through the rigging and shrouds!

SAVED.

There was just a morsel of a moon, but it was seldom seen for the black drifting clouds. It must be nigh midnight, thought those storm-tossed sailors. All hands were on deck. No bells were struck, nor could a watch be looked at. Suddenly, during a temporary gleam of moonlight, a blacker cloud than any yet seen appeared on the horizon. Every *old* sailor knew what that cloud was—a wall of beetling cliffs.

"Ready about?"

Yes, but it was too late. Next moment she had struck with fearful violence, and reeling back tottered and began to sink.

Boat after boat was lowered, only to be smashed to pieces.

One was safely got away from the sinking ship, and steered for lights they could see to the left. A signal was fired. A blue light burned. Lights were seen waving on shore as if to encourage them.

They are close in shore, among the awful surf. Can they do it? The night got clearer far now. There was a good show of moonlight on the water and the light from the foam itself. When it seemed as almost impossible the boat could reach the shore, a dozen hardy fishermen rushed into the sea, the painter was thrown to them and grasped, and next moment they were safe, though wholly exhausted.

Morning broke immediately after, showing how much they had been mistaken in thinking it but midnight when the vessel struck. But time flies quickly, even in danger, when one is busy.

The shipwrecked men—the few saved—were kindly cared for. Harvey found himself inside a curious and humble dwelling, tended by the funniest little old man he had ever seen. The house was made out of a boat. The funny little old man was our old friend Duncan Reed.

Duncan, next day, told him a wondrous deal about the glen and about Kenneth's old friends, all of which were duly chronicled in Harvey's mind, and in due time found their way in writing to his comrades beyond the sea.

They say that possession is nine points of the law; this does not hold good, however, in the case, say, of a thief being caught with a dozen silver spoons in his pocket.

"Might is right" is another common saying, but neither the might of wealth nor the fact of his being in possession of the Alva estate prevented Mr Steve, the millionaire, having finally to leave it.

When the news of McGregor's success came, the rejoicing in the clachan and the glens was such as had never been remembered before. Bonfires blazed on every hill. Lads and lasses danced, old men wrung each other by the hands, and old wives wept for joy.

Old Duncan is even reported to have danced a hornpipe.

Poor Duncan! he was offered a kindly home at the mansion of Alva.

"It is mindful of you, sir," old Duncan replied, "but out o' sight of the sea, out o' hearin' o' the waves, Duncan wouldna live a week. I'll lay my bones beside her soon."

Chapter Twenty Four
In the "Fa' o' the Year"

"'Mid pleasures and palaces where'er we may roam,
Be it ever so humble, there's no place like home."

Old Song.

"Fareweel, fareweel, my native hame,
Thy lonely glens and heath-clad mountains;
Fareweel thy fields o' storied fame,
Thy leafy shaws and sparklin' fountains."

A. Hume.

Scene: Glen Alva. Down in the clachan and lowlands, and around the mansion house, the autumnal tints are on the trees; the chestnuts, the lime and the maples have turned a rich yellow, and soon the leaves will fall; but the elm and oak retain their sturdy green. So do the waving pines. High on the hillsides the heather still blooms. There is silence almost everywhere to-day. Silence on mountain and silence in forest. Only the sweet plaintive twitter of the robin is heard in garden and copse. He sings the dirge of the departed summer. It is indeed the "fa' o' the year."

Time: Five years have elapsed since the date of the events described in last chapter.

In my humble opinion—and I daresay many coincide with me—the great poet never spoke truer words than these:—

"There's a Divinity that shapes our lives, Rough-hew them as we will."

Who could have thought that Harvey McGregor, with his fearless nature, his tameless spirit, and roaming disposition, would ever have settled down in quiet Glen Alva, or that Kenneth McAlpine would have developed into a farmer in the Far West.

But so, indeed, it was.

Ambition—well guided—is a noble thing. All my three heroes were ambitious. Harvey's ambition, perhaps, was tinctured with some degree of pride. He fought long and manfully for fortune, and when he fell, he had the grace to own it. Kenneth's and Archie's ambition was more to be admired, and I love the man or boy who has a feeling of independence in his breast, and who, if he should fail in one line of life, turns cheerfully to another, with a determination to do his duty, and never give up. Dost remember the lines of the good poet Tupper? They are better than many a hymn, and may help to cheer you in hours when life seems dark and hopeless.

> "Never give up! It is wiser and better
>   Always to hope, than once to despair;
> Fling off the load of Doubt's heavy fetter,
>   And break the dark spell of tyrannical Care.
> Never give up! or the burden may sink you,
>   Providence kindly has mingled the cup;
> And in all trials and troubles, bethink you,
>   The watchword of life must be, Never give up!
> Never give up, there are chances and changes,
>   Helping the hopeful, a hundred to one,
> And through the chaos High Wisdom arranges
>   Ever success,—if you'll only hope on.
> Never give up! for the wisest is boldest,
>   Knowing that Providence mingles the cup,

And of all maxims the best, as the oldest,
Is the true watchword of Never give up."

SCENE IN GLEN ALVA.

Yes, ambition is a noble thing; yet it should not be a selfish ambition. Blessed is he who works and toils and struggles for the happiness of the masses, as well as for his own. Has not He Who spoke as never man spake left us a glorious example to follow—follow, if only afar off?

But now let us take a peep into the tartan parlour of Alva House, a peep at the fireside life of young Laird McGregor, on this quiet autumnal afternoon.

When we were introduced into this same parlour, we found it the scene of a revel, over which it is as well to draw the curtain of oblivion.

But now, here are seated Harvey McGregor and his young wife. Yes, he is married, and a babe has come to bless him, too.

Near the fire, in a high-backed chair, is Harvey's mother. She looks very contented, and there are smiles chasing each other all round her lips and eyes.

But where, think you, is baby? On his mother's lap, you say? Nay, but positively on his father's knee—his father, the quondam rover of the sea and the prairies.

It is somewhat absurd, I grant you, but there is no getting over facts. Sometimes brave soldiers or sailors make the best of fireside folks, when they *do* settle down.

And Harvey McGregor is not only nursing his young heir, but he is actually nodding at him and talking sweet nonsense to him, while baby crows, and Harvey's wife looks on delightedly.

So busily are all engaged that they do not hear the hall door bell ring, nor know anything at all about its being rung either, until suddenly a Highland servant enters with two cards on a tray.

Harvey hands baby to his mother in some confusion—I'm not at all sure he did not blush a little; but no sooner has he taken the cards and read them, than he jumps up from his chair as if a hornet had stung him.

"Hurrah!" he cries.

"Dear me, Harvey! what is it?" his wife exclaims.

"Nothing, my dear," says Harvey; "that is—it is everything, I mean. It is joy in the house of McGregor. Hurrah!"

And away he rushes, leaving his wife and mother to wonder.

They were in the library, the pair of them. They had not even sat down, because they knew Harvey would soon come.

And they were not mistaken.

"Why, Kenneth! Archie!" he cried, extending a hand to each, "my dear old shipmates, 'pals,' and partners, how are you?"

"Took you by surprise, eh?" replied Kenneth, laughing.

"Why, the biggest and the best surprise I've had for many a day. But how are you? and where have you come from last? and how goes the farm out in the West?"

Harvey put a dozen other questions, but he gave his friends no time to answer one.

I leave my readers to guess whether or not they spent a pleasant, happy evening together. Ay, and not one, but many. For Harvey was not going to let them go for a long time, you may be sure. So they stayed on and on for weeks. There was plenty of sport and fun to be got all day, but, nevertheless, the evenings were always most pleasant. There was so much to talk about, and so much to tell each other, that time fled on swallows' wings, and it was always pretty near the—

"Wee short 'oor ayout the twal,"

before they parted for the night.

Need I say that one of the first places visited by Kenneth and Archie—and they stole away all alone—was Kooran's grave, and the fairy knoll? They were delighted to find the former carefully kept, and quite surprised to find the latter completely furnished. The inside was a cave no longer, except in shape. It was a library, a boudoir, call it what you may.

"How mindful of dear Harvey!" said Kenneth.

"Yes, indeed," replied Archie; "and think, too, of his goodness to my dear father, of the comfortable house he dwells in, and the smiling little croft around it."

"Harvey," said Kenneth with enthusiasm, "is one of Nature's noblemen.

> "'Away with false fashion, so calm and so chill,
> Where pleasure itself cannot please;
> Away with cold breeding, that faithlessly still
> Affects to be quite at its ease.
> For the deepest in feeling is highest in rank,
> The freest is first of the band:
> And Nature's own nobleman, friendly and frank,
> Is the man with his heart in his hand.'"

"Come, I say, Kennie, my learned old man, when you are talking poetry, and such ringing verses, too, as these, I dare say you imagine I must sing small; but bide a wee, lad, there is two of us can play at the same game. What say you if I match Burns against your Tupper? Hear then."

And, with figure and head erect, with arms extended and open palm, Archie spoke,—

"Is there for honest poverty,
That hangs his head and a' that?
The coward-slave, we pass him by,
And dare be poor for a' that.
What though on homely fare we dine,
Wear hodden-grey (coarse, woollen, undyed cloth) and a'
that, Give fools their silks, and knaves their wine,
A man's a man for a' that.

"A prince can make a belted knight,
A marquis, duke and a' that;
But an honest man's above his might,
Guid faith he mauna fa' that. (Try.)
Then let us pray that come it may,
As come it will for a' that,
That sense and worth o'er a' the earth,
May bear the gree for a' that."

(Bear the gree, *i.e.*, be triumphant.)

"Bravo! Archie, lad. Glad to see that you haven't forgotten your Scotch, though we've talked little but English for many a long day.

"Ah! well," he continued, after a pause, "I was just thinking, Archie, how kind Providence has been to us."

"But mind you, Kenneth, we've worked hard."

"ONE TERRIBLE NIGHT AT SEA."

"I'm not saying we haven't, Archie, I'm not saying we haven't. We *have* worked; and I say shame on the sheep who huddles down in a corner and nurses himself, and thinks that Heaven will give him every blessing for the asking. We must work as well as pray."

"Do you know, Archie, that one terrible night at sea, while we were rounding the Horn with a whole gale of wind blowing and a smothering sea on, when it was so dark you couldn't have seen a sheet of white paper held at arm's length, and when we all of a sudden knew from the frightful cold we were surrounded by ice, when at last the ship was struck and began to leak, and no one had a hope of seeing the morn break—that down below I stole just one half minute to open my Book? And my eyes fell upon the ninety-first Psalm, and I took comfort and heart at once; I knew we would be saved, and next day the captain complimented me on having been so daring, so fearless, and cheerful. Ah! lad, little did he know that the bravery in my breast was no bravery of mine; it *had been put there by Him*. Call this faith of mine folly if you like, I don't care; it suits *me*, and it has saved me more than once, and comforted me a thousand times.

"Do you mind the time," Kenneth went on, changing the subject, "when you and I used to herd the sheep here with dear old Kooran and Shot?"

"Can I e'er forget it, Kenneth?"

Sitting on the top of the fairy knoll there, the two young men had quite a long talk about bygone times. I have said "young men;" and they were so, though they might not have appeared to be in the eyes of boys and girls, but as they talked they seemed to grow younger still. Kenneth could almost imagine he saw the smoke curling up from his mother's cot in the glen, and Kooran feathering away through the heather to fetch his dinner. (See Book One, chapter one.)

A day or two after this the three friends went together over the hills to pay a visit to the fisherman's cot by the beach.

Duncan Reed was so glad to see them. He was not so very much altered in appearance. They found him seated in the sunlight, with a very large Bible on his lap, and an immense pair of hornrimmed spectacles on his nose.

Duncan drops out of the story here. He is gone years ago. Suffice it to say he had his wish—he sleeps beside the sea.

On their return journey they visited the ruins of old Nancy Dobbell's cottage. Harvey McGregor made one remark which explains much.

"That old woman," he said, "alone knew my secret."

Passing onwards towards the forest, Kenneth ventured to ask for the first time about Jessie Grant.

"Heigho!" replied Harvey; "I cared not to mention it in my letter, but that family were in reduced circumstances even before the father and mother died; now poor Jessie lives at Helensburgh in a humble cottage with her aunt."

"And she is not—"

"No, not married."

A thrill of joy went through Kenneth's heart. It was not unaccompanied by a kind of satisfied feeling of pride. He could not quite forget the time when proud Mr Redmond offered him the position of ghillie on his premises.

Need I say that Kenneth soon found Jessie out? She was more beautiful than ever in his eyes.

Archie and Kenneth took rooms at Helensburgh—for sake of the fishing. At least Kenneth said it was for sake of the fishing; but he did not look Archie quite straight in the face when he made the remark.

When, after a few weeks, Kenneth proposed marriage to Jessie, his offer was—refused.

Why? Truth to tell, Jessie loved him, but she said to herself, "Now he is rich and I am poor, it cannot be."

I do not know whether this was a pardonable pride in Jessie or not. Perhaps it was.

Then came an evening when Kenneth, Archie, and Jessie were strolling together on the banks of the loch. It was to be the last night in Scotland of the two American farmers, as they called themselves, and she could not refuse to go with them to see the sun set behind the mountains.

Kenneth felt very sad, and spoke but little, Jessie hardly at all; in fact, she felt that it would not take much to make her cry.

Archie was still a student of natural history, and a new species of fern caught his eye. He must climb the fence, must commit a trespass even to find it, and his companions strolled on.

It was hardly an evening calculated to inspire hope or joy. A breeze roughened the lake, and went moaning through the almost leafless trees; the fields were bare or ploughed, the hedgerows looked sickly, and the brackens—so lovely in summer—were brown or broken down or bent. Still, the robin sang in the woods. That was something.

Kenneth and Jessie leant against a stile to wait for Archie; but that fern required a deal of examination.

"Archie seems in no hurry," said Jessie, looking back.

"He has found a flower of some kind, I suppose," replied Kenneth.

"There are few flowers in November," she said, quickly.

"Here are two. Do you remember them, Miss Redmond?" As he spoke he produced old Nancy's Bible, and opened it.

The flowers were there, but sadly withered.

This is precisely the remark that Jessie made.

"I do," she said, with a blush and a sigh; "but they are sadly withered."

"Like my hopes," replied Kenneth. "I leave my country a broken-hearted man—"

How handy for an author is a line of those little stars called "asterisks!" How neatly I dropped the curtain by means of it on that conversation between Kenneth and Jessie!

But *did* Kenneth leave his country a broken-hearted man? No; how could he with Jessie by his side?

They were married at Alva House by old Mr Grant. It was a quiet wedding indoors, but out of doors—well, Harvey McGregor determined his tenantry should all go mad together if they chose. There were balls and bonfires, breakfasts, dinners, and suppers *galore*, and such rejoicing and such general jollity as will never be forgotten while the heather blooms on Alva hills, and the dark pines wave in its valleys.

The honeymoon was spent in the New Forest; and Kenneth did not forget to visit his old friend Major Walton, whom he found happy and hearty.

Beautiful are the farms that Kenneth and Archie occupy in far-off British Columbia. There is a thriving village near them now, and churches and schools; but their farms lie well in the outskirts. What though in winter wild winds wail around the dwellings, and shake the pine trees on the mountain sides? there are warmth and light and brightness indoors; and some laughing and fun, too, for there are children, one, two, three; and Uncle Archie, as the latter call him, drops in nearly every evening to spend an hour or two, so no one thinks the time long.

Then in summer, oh! to roam in those beautiful woods, and cull the fruit and the wild flowers. And at this sweet time of the year, the gardens and lawns and terraces, and the verandahs of Kenneth's many-gabled dwelling, are bathed in floral beauty. It is quite a sight to see, and to dream about ever afterwards.

And no one, I think, would begrudge Kenneth his happiness. He worked for it.

Good-bye, reader.